ACCLAIM FOR
TO ENCHANT A LADY'S HEART

"Hatcher's newest novella offers the same sweet romance and page-turning storyline you've come to expect from this author if you've read her before. If you haven't, you're in for a treat! *To Enchant a Lady's Heart* is, in a word, well...*enchanting.*"
— Deborah Raney, author of *Breath of Heaven* and *A Nest of Sparrows*

"Robin Lee Hatcher opens her new series, The British Are Coming, with a delightful novella that's sure to capture readers' hearts. The characters are unique, and the plot is engaging from start to finish. This promises to be a fun series with a clash of cultures as the British characters travel to the Western United States. Readers who are looking for well written historical romance will enjoy this novella and the novels to follow."
— Carrie Turansky, award-winning author of *No Journey Too Far* and *The Legacy of Longdale Manor*

"A sweet romance set against the backdrop of lovely Victorian England countryside, along with the era's not-so-lovely convention that mandated a woman of means agree to an arranged marriage. But as we quickly discover, Eliza Southwick is no ordinary woman! Grab a cup of hot tea and a plush throw, and curl up to savor *To Enchant a Lady's Heart*, the delightful novella launching Robin Lee Hatcher's newest series, The British are Coming!"

— Tamera Alexander, *USA Today* bestselling author of *Colors of Truth*

"Such a sweet, engaging story! I fell in love with spunky Amanda, goodhearted Adam, and dear Eliza who longed to be seen for herself and not for what her father's wealth could bring to the table. I enjoyed every minute of my time at Hooke Manor and look forward to a return visit in Sebastian's story."

— Kim Vogel Sawyer, bestselling author of *Still My Forever*

"May I break the rules and give this novella six stars? The extra star is for the chance to sit down, read a story all the way through in that one sitting, and come away very satisfied by the ending. Robin Lee Hatcher has improved her serve—and she has served a winning, intelligent, and gripping book. I'll read this one again!"

— Hannah Alexander, author of *A Killing Frost*

"I love Regency and Victorian romances, and Robin Lee Hatcher's *To Enchant a Lady's Heart* didn't disappoint. It was great fun to follow Eliza and Adam's growing love in spite of all the strict social protocols of that time period and at the same time see the setup for Robin's new series, The British Are Coming. Sit back and enjoy! I guarantee you'll be glad you did."
— Gayle Roper, *Lost and Found, Hide and Seek*

"Love the prospect of connection from England to the Old West in the 1890s. This should make a wonderful historical romance TV series. In the midst of stringent times of London's titled society's mores for women and illegitimate children, examples of grace shown in surprising quarters. Also, appreciated the spiritual applications made in growth of relationships and testing of faith."
— Janet Chester Bly, author of the Trails of Reba Cahill Series

"*To Enchant A Lady's Heart* is filled with rich history and charming characters. Hatcher delivers an inspirational romance that will once again enchant readers."
— New York Times Bestselling Author, Rachel Hauck

To Enchant a Lady's Heart

THE BRITISH ARE COMING
BOOK ONE

ROBIN LEE HATCHER

With thanks to those who have encouraged me in a new season of life, especially to Jim B., Deb R., and Creston M.

"Two are better than one because they have a good return for their labor. For if either of them falls, the one will lift up his companion. But woe to the one who falls when there is not another to lift him up." (Ecclesiastes 4:9–10, NASB95)

Prologue

The Blakeslee ballroom glittered as couples swirled around the dance floor. Laughter and voices rose above the music, creating a loud din.

Standing alone, not far from the refreshments, Eliza Southwick observed the festive gathering and wished herself back home at Briar Park. Her new ballgown was too tight across the shoulders, and her dancing slippers pinched her toes. No longer a young debutante, she wasn't eagerly sought after by the eligible men in attendance. That might have stung if she'd met a gentleman she found interesting. She hadn't. Not at this ball nor any other she'd attended since her introduction to society.

She covered her mouth with a gloved hand, hiding a yawn of boredom behind it.

The official London Season had ended over two

1

months ago, but people always returned to the city for Lord and Lady Blakeslee's Autumn Ball. Even Eliza's father wouldn't have missed it, especially not while he had hopes that his daughter would capture the attention of a titled lord.

Looking away from the dance floor, she caught sight of her father, deep in conversation with the Earl of Hooke, Lord Whitcombe. The earl had an unmarried son. She'd met Sebastian Whitcombe on more than one occasion, and she liked him well enough. But she didn't think they would suit each other. For one thing, Sebastian didn't seem to share her passion for horses nor did he seem to like reading, another of her interests. Did her father know that about him? Did he know it about her? Did he care?

She closed her eyes as she stepped closer to a large parlor palm. Behind her, rain still splattered against the windows, but she couldn't hear it falling now. She wished she could, for it was a sound that soothed her when she felt uncertain…and unloved.

A memory flitted through her mind. The memory of an evening in the stables at Briar Park several months ago and of the man who had waited and watched with her while a foal was born.

Dear God, please send the right man into my life. Please send me someone to love.

Chapter One

Hooke Manor
Winter 1895

T he earl wishes to see you in the library, Mr.
Faulkner. At once."

Without comment, Adam gave the black mare a pat
on the shoulder, then left the stall, following the young
footman out of the stables and toward one of the rear
entrances to the manor house. He leaned into the bitter
wind that sliced through his coat, all the while wishing
he'd gone to London with Sebastian that morning.
Anything would be better than what awaited him in the
library. The Earl of Hooke had been in a foul temper
for days, and there was only one reason he'd sent for
Adam now. He wanted help, the sort of help Adam
didn't want to give.

Once inside the manor, he went straight to the
library. He didn't remove his coat or take time to wash

up. The earl was not a patient man in the best of circumstances.

"You sent for me, my lord." Adam stopped inside the doorway.

An imposing man in his late sixties with steel gray hair and eyes, the earl paced back and forth in front of a stone fireplace. Finally he stopped and glared in Adam's direction. "You knew Sebastian went to London?"

"Yes, my lord. He told me before he left." Adam paused before adding, "He asked me to go with him. He wanted to open his house."

"Blast that boy."

Sebastian Whitcombe, Viscount Willowthorpe, was not a boy. Adam's half-brother was in his early thirties.

"Why didn't you stop him?" the earl demanded. "You know we have guests arriving tomorrow."

"Yes, my lord. I know. But he was determined."

"Blast." The older man spun toward the blazing fire. "It's time he settled down and married. It's time he had children of his own. He has a duty to this family, to Hooke Manor."

Adam said nothing. When the earl was like this, no words were required. In truth, prudence demanded silence.

The earl gripped the mantel with both hands and leaned closer to the fire, his entire body rigid. After a long, silent spell, he drew a deep breath and faced Adam again. "I'll see that he returns home at once."

"Do you want me to go to London?"

"No." The earl shook his head. "No, I want you to stay here. We have guests arriving. *I* will go to London. I

6

have things to say to my son that must be said in person. You will stay here and assist Amanda with our guests."

"You want me to assist?"

"Yes. Sebastian and I will return on Wednesday, well before the rest of our guests arrive. But Lord George and his daughter will be here tomorrow. I don't want Amanda to face them alone."

Uncomfortable as he was at the thought, Adam answered, "As you wish, my lord."

The earl sighed. "Why couldn't that boy be more like you?" He turned to the fireplace, and by his demeanor, Adam knew he'd been dismissed.

The earl was wrong, of course. Sebastian and Adam were more similar than their father acknowledged. They looked enough alike to be full brothers, and once, over a decade earlier, they'd been mistaken for twins, despite the three years that separated them. In addition to their similar looks, they had matching senses of humor and enjoyed riding fast horses.

There was, however, a not-so-small difference between the half-brothers. Sebastian was a gentleman and the heir to the earldom while Adam had been born on the wrong side of the blanket.

Another difference was Sebastian's reluctance to marry. Especially to marry someone deemed suitable by their father. Unfortunately, the young woman their father had chosen for Sebastian had captured a piece of Adam's heart months ago, a fact he had revealed to no one.

Why would he reveal it? He couldn't act upon his feelings, no matter how much he would like to. He was, after all, the illegitimate son of the Earl of Hooke. He'd been treated kindly since coming to live at the manor at the age of four. In many ways he'd been treated as an equal to Sebastian. He'd received an education. He'd become the stable manager while still in his twenties, and his income was generous. In the right setting, he was accepted by Sebastian's closest friends with nary a disapproving glance.

And yet Adam knew his place.

There was also the matter of Eliza's dowry, not to mention the stallion she would bring to Hooke Manor. The earl wanted the dowry, of course, but he coveted the horse. And to get them both Sebastian must marry Miss Southwick.

As Adam returned to the stables, he reminded himself that his half-brother was a good man. Sebastian might not want to marry Eliza at present, but he would grow to care for her, given a little time. How could he help it once he stopped objecting simply because their father liked her?

There was so much to like about Eliza Southwick, too. She was pretty in an unconventional way. Petite and curvaceous, she had a heart-shaped face, dark hair, and a musical laugh. But it was the sparkle of mischief in her eyes that had drawn Adam's attention the previous year. That and a passion for horses that matched his own.

In fact, it was horses that had caused them to meet. Eliza had slipped away from the guests at the Briar Park house party to visit the stables where a favorite mare was about to foal. Adam had been in the stables as well, attending to the Whitcombe horses. Moonlight had ushered Eliza through the open stable door, silvering the gown she'd worn. She'd looked like an angel, and Adam had never recovered.

He gave his head a quick shake, driving away the memory. He couldn't continue to think about Eliza that way. Not if she was to be Sebastian's bride. And that would surely happen. The earl didn't give up on a plan once his mind was set.

Countess—the mare he'd been attending earlier and one of the finest horses on his father's estate—greeted Adam with a huff of air and the stomp of a hoof. He ran a hand along the mare's back but found it difficult to focus his thoughts on the animal. They kept wandering to Sebastian…and to Miss Eliza Southwick. Frustrated, he turned and gave instructions to the stable boy who waited nearby. Then Adam left the horse barn, this time going to his small cottage, wishing he could drown his thoughts in a bottle of spirits but knowing instead that he would spend a long evening staring into the fire, filled with regret.

WEAK MORNING SUNLIGHT spilled through the windows of the bedchamber as Eliza stared at the looking glass. But she took no note of her reflection therein. Her thoughts were instead upon her father and the days ahead of her.

At twenty-four, Eliza was beyond the age when her father, the third son of the Marquis of Heathborough, had expected her to make an appropriate match. Society agreed. Too many London Seasons had passed for her to be taken seriously by most gentlemen in search of a wife. They viewed her as unwanted goods, despite the wealth of her father, Lord George Southwick. No man had proposed to her in her first season or those that followed. Her own fault for keeping them at bay. So why should any man choose her now? There were too many younger, more beautiful girls to choose from with each new year.

Eliza wondered what her father had offered the Earl of Hooke to make her desirable enough for a match with Viscount Willowthorpe. The price must be exceedingly high.

Tears pooled in her eyes. She would like nothing more than to marry, but she so wished it could be for love. If not love, respect. Or at the very least that a man might want her for herself and not to improve his purse or his riding stables.

"Miss?"

She blinked away the unshed tears before turning toward the door.

Her maid stepped into the room. "Your father says for you to come at once. Are you ready?"

"I am, Mary. Thank you." She retrieved her gloves from a nearby table and tugged them onto her hands. Then she pointed to a bag. "That is the last one."

"I'll see to it."

Head held high, Eliza made her way along the hallway and down the stairs to the main entrance where her father waited, impatience in his eyes. He gave her a quick, appraising look. Apparently she passed the inspection for he gave a curt nod and turned to lead the way outside.

Patches of snow from a rare late winter storm lingered beneath trees and in the shadows of buildings, and a cold wind assaulted Eliza as she followed her father to the carriage. The gusts cut through her cloak like a knife. She would be thankful for the blankets and furs inside the coach, but despite them, she knew she would be chilled to the bone before they reached Hooke Manor in the afternoon. She shuddered to think what it would be like for their servants who had to make the journey in the elements. At least her maid and her father's valet would be inside the second coach that carried all of their luggage. Luggage packed with enough clothing to last them for a variety of occasions for more than a week. Assuming everything went as her father planned, Eliza would need each and every ensemble.

George Southwick was not one to engage in idle conversation if it could be avoided, so Eliza was left to her own thoughts as they set off across the countryside. Those thoughts, despite her best efforts to thwart them, settled immediately on Sebastian Whitcombe. Without question, the viscount was handsome, and the times she'd been in his company, she'd found him charming and engaging. All of the other unmarried females in England felt the same about him, no doubt.

So why would he want to marry Eliza?

Again, she wondered what her father had offered for his only daughter, above and beyond the expected dowry. And that made her feel like a horse at auction. A rather pathetic view of herself, she supposed, especially since the arrangement was not unusual. It was the way things had been done among the aristocracy for centuries. Marriages were more often about position and money rather than affection. Marrying for love had never been the expected practice for those of rank. Perhaps not for commoners either.

If only Mother were alive to help me sort this out.

She closed her eyes, picturing her mother. Gwendolyn Southwick had been more than a great beauty. Exuding elegance and grace, she had also possessed a gentle and kind spirit, beloved by all who knew her but especially by her daughter. Eliza had been only ten when her mother died while giving birth to William, the surviving son and heir to the Southwick estate. It seemed to Eliza that she'd ceased to exist at that same moment her mother passed away.

Looking across the carriage at her father, she felt the sadness in her chest increase. He wasn't cruel to her. Only indifferent. And that cut deeper than cruelty. She was, after all, a daughter and not a son. Her role was to marry well. It mattered little whether she was happy.

Chapter Two

As expected, Eliza felt half-frozen by the time the Southwick carriage arrived at Hooke Manor. Despite the cold, staff members stood outside to welcome Lord George Southwick and his daughter. Adam Faulkner was there as well. However, the earl and his heir were noticeably absent.

"My apologies, Lord George," Adam said. "Lord Whitcombe and Lord Sebastian made an unexpected trip to London. They hope to return in the morning. The earl asked that I extend you and your daughter every courtesy."

From beneath her lashes, Eliza studied Adam as he addressed her father. She wondered if he remembered meeting her the previous summer. She also noted that he'd claimed no relation to the rest of the Whitcombe family, although she knew he was, indeed, related. But a relation without legal rights. Adam Faulkner had been given a home at Hooke Manor after his unfortunate mother died of consumption when he was four. Or so Eliza had been told by her maid.

At one time it had surprised her how well informed Mary was about the inhabitants of other great houses, both upstairs and down. That was no longer the case. She'd learned the staff seemed to know everything about everyone. A good thing to remember should she ever have any secrets of her own. For if her maid knew all the gossip, so would the maids of other ladies. Her secrets included.

"Eliza," her father said firmly, pulling her from her reverie. Only then did she realize Adam Faulkner had addressed her.

She returned his greeting. He smiled, and something warmed inside of her. He looked a great deal like his half-brother, but his eyes were so much friendlier. He seemed to actually *see* her. Then he turned to address a servant, allowing the cold to sweep through her again.

A short while later, Eliza was led to an upstairs bedchamber that was nearly twice the size of hers at home. Mary awaited her there. Soon she was seated beside a blazing fire with a shawl over her knees and a hot drink between her hands.

"Are you disappointed, Miss Eliza?"

She glanced at her maid. "Disappointed?"

"That Lord Willowthorpe wasn't here to greet you. The viscount is the reason you've come, after all."

"There is nothing to be done if he was called away." In truth, she was relieved. She wouldn't mind another day or two before having her life arranged by others.

Mary said, "It is a grand house, miss."

"Yes, it is grand."

"Imagine being the lady of the manor."

"Yes, imagine," she whispered as she subdued a shudder.

Eliza would so much rather live a quiet life than reign over a house like Hooke Manor or Briar Park. But she could never tell her father how she felt. Nor could she tell any of her friends. None of them would understand.

"Would you like to lie down before dressing for supper?"

"No, thank you, Mary. I will stay by the fire. That's enough of a rest, I think."

"As you wish, miss." The maid withdrew.

Once Eliza was somewhat warmer, she rose from the chair and placed the shawl about her shoulders. Then she walked to one of the windows to look out at the grounds beyond the glass. The day was gray and blustery. The trees at the far end of the expansive gardens were devoid of leaves. Still, she thought, everything must be beautiful in the summer when there were flowers in bloom and the fountain sprayed water.

"But does anyone enjoy it?" she asked aloud.

Eliza knew that the earl's second wife had passed away after a lengthy illness. But what of Sebastian's younger sister? Adam Faulkner hadn't mentioned her. Surely if Lady Amanda was at Hooke Manor, she would have been the one to welcome their guests.

Feeling restless, Eliza decided a walk was in order. However, she had no desire to go outside into the cold. She would explore the house instead. Could anyone blame her for wanting a closer look? Especially if she was destined to become mistress of it.

She left the bedchamber and made her way down the main staircase. The grand salon, spacious and elegant, was the first room at the bottom of the stairs. She noted the large portrait of the present earl above the fireplace. It was an honest likeness of the man, which made her wonder about the artist. Most portraits flattered their subjects. This artist had been bold, and she liked him for it, whoever he was.

The next room she entered was the dining hall. The long table had enough seating for at least forty people. Overhead, stretching the full length of the room, was a row of chandeliers. The wood surface of the table shone in the pale light falling through the windows, and there was a faint lemon scent in the air that announced servants had been polishing not that long ago.

The drawing room bore a woman's touch, and Eliza immediately knew this would be her favorite room should the desired match come to pass. Clusters of chairs filled the room, giving it an intimate feeling. And the many windows must let in light from early morning well into the afternoon on a sunny day. Yes, it would be her favorite room, without doubt.

Across the hall, she discovered the music room, a Steinway grand piano its focal point. Amanda Whitcombe probably played beautifully. Eliza had little talent for musical instruments. She hoped she would not be asked to perform during this visit.

In all of her wandering, she saw no one. It seemed as if she had the entire manor to herself, although she knew it wasn't true. One servant or another must have observed her while she explored the main floor. But it wasn't until she was in the long hallway on the north side of the house, studying the portraits there, that she heard footsteps, announcing the presence of another. She turned, expecting to find the butler or the house-keeper or perhaps a footman. Instead, she discovered Adam Faulkner walking toward her.

"Miss Southwick," he said when he stopped.

"Mr. Faulkner." She nodded, her pulse quickening, as if she'd been caught misbehaving.

Eliza Southwick was every bit as lovely as Adam remembered.

"I hope you don't mind that I have been exploring your house," she said, coloring slightly.

It wasn't his house, of course, but he didn't correct her. "Not at all. Is this your first visit to Hooke Manor?"

"Yes. And as you know, it is ever so much more grand than Briar Park."

"Larger, perhaps, but your father's stables are finer."

A sparkle entered her eyes. "Are they?"

"Indeed." He smiled. "Would you care to compare? I have the advantage since I've seen the stables at Briar Park."

The color returned to her cheeks. "I remember, Mr. Faulkner."

It pleased him that she did.

"I would like to see your stables, if it is not too much trouble."

"Not at all." He offered his arm. "Let's get your wrap."

A short while later, Adam and Eliza followed the path to the stables. When they were inside, Eliza lowered the hood of her cloak. A lock of dark hair fell loose from its pinnings to curl against her nape, and Adam had to fight the urge to reach out and sweep it aside. And perhaps kiss that spot.

He cleared his throat as he stepped away from her. "Let me introduce you to Countess." He walked to the mare's stall. At the same time, the horse thrust her head over the door and nickered.

"Oh!"

Adam smiled, pleased by her reaction. "Grand, isn't she?"

"Oh my, yes." She arrived at Adam's side. "How could you say my father's stables are finer? Look at her. She's gorgeous." She stroked the horse's head.

"Countess is his lordship's favorite."

As if in agreement, the horse snorted and bobbed her head.

Eliza laughed, and the sound was like a melody that reached inside Adam and wound around his heart, stealing his breath away. For an instant, he resented his half-brother. If their father had married Adam's mother, Adam would be the eldest son. He would be the heir. He would be the one destined to marry Eliza Southwick.

"Come with me, Miss Southwick." The words sounded gruff in his own ears, and he cleared his throat to try to disguise it. "I'll show you the rest of the horses."

At each subsequent stall, she asked questions. About training. About feeding practices. Even about breeding. And by her questions, she revealed her own knowledge of horses. A knowledge far above most young women of her station.

He was tempted to turn the questions in her direction. He would love to ask about the stallion she would bring with her to the manor if and when she married Sebastian. But prudence kept him silent.

They had nearly completed their tour of the stables when a blast of cold air hit them. Adam looked in the direction of the door to find George Southwick in the opening. His gaze dismissed Adam as unimportant before settling on his daughter. "I thought this was where I would find you." Displeasure colored his voice.

"I'm sorry, Father. I didn't know you would look for me before supper." She glanced at Adam. "Mr. Faulkner was kind enough to show me Lord Whitcombe's stables."

Her eyes seemed to apologize. But it was the sadness in their depths that Adam noticed. Another temptation pulled at him. This time to comfort her. He didn't care at all what her father thought of him. He'd experienced judgment before and knew there was little he could do about it. He couldn't change the nature of his birth. But he did care that something or someone had hurt Eliza.

Her father held out his hand and waved for her to join him.

"Thank you, Mr. Faulkner," she said softly, then

raised her hood, covering her head, and hurried to her father. A moment later, they strode from view.

Adam shoved down the welling disappointment as he crossed to the door and closed it. Served him right. He shouldn't spend time alone with Eliza. Not feeling as he did about her. Then again, his father had asked him to see to their guests, and she'd wanted to explore the stables. Good manners wouldn't have allowed him to do anything else.

"God help me," he whispered. "Not even I believe that excuse."

Chapter Three

When Eliza entered the dining room that evening, she was surprised to find Amanda Whitcombe standing with her half-brother near one of the fireplaces.

"Miss Southwick, how good to see you." Amanda moved toward her. "I apologize for being absent when you arrived this afternoon, but I'm sure Adam gave you a proper welcome." She glanced over her shoulder.

Adam responded with a half-smile.

Eliza waited for him to meet her eyes, but instead, he turned away. "Excuse me, ladies." He left the room.

"Don't mind him. A servant brought news that one of the horses has been injured. He will return as soon as he is able." Amanda took Eliza's arm and drew her to the end of the long table where four place settings were lit by candlelight. "Now tell me. How have you been since I saw you last?"

Lady Amanda Whitcombe was everything Eliza

wished she could be—vivacious, classically beautiful, and witty. Suitors had flocked to Amanda's side since her first season. If rumors were true, she had turned down more than one proposal of marriage. It surprised Eliza that the earl hadn't insisted she accept one of those offers. Her own father would have done so.

Sadly, Eliza had no offers, and now her father had to bribe someone to take her off his hands.

She pushed down the unpleasant thought, determined not to let it rise again. She should be glad for the prospect of marriage to someone like Sebastian, for more reasons than she cared to list. At the very least because he wasn't old and infirm or a cruel ogre.

"Has it been a year already?" Amanda asked lightly.

Eliza was about to answer but was interrupted by the arrival of her father. Amanda performed her duties as hostess, all with a smile that disarmed even George Southwick.

"Adam was called away," Amanda said at last, "but he insisted that we not wait supper on him."

"I should think not." Eliza's father looked appalled.

With an easy charm, Amanda hooked her arm through his. "You must not think ill of us, Lord George. We must seem ill-prepared for your visit, with my father and Sebastian rushing off to town at the last minute, and Adam being called away to manage things on the estate. However, I assure you, we have all looked forward to your coming." Her glance flicked to Eliza. "And to seeing your lovely daughter once again."

Her father seemed somewhat mollified by Amanda's

words, and he allowed her to draw him to the table without resistance.

During the meal, Eliza couldn't help but admire their hostess. Amanda guided the conversation from one topic to another with ease. It was plain that Eliza's father had fallen under Amanda's spell. Eliza could have slipped from the dining room, and her father wouldn't have noticed.

She was wishing she could do exactly that when Adam appeared in the doorway. Dressed for dinner, his manner seemed more reserved and formal than it had earlier in the day. But his lingering gaze caused Eliza's heart to flutter as he took his place across from her.

"I hope the horse is all right," she said to him.

He smiled briefly. "I believe he will be, Miss Southwick. Thank you for inquiring."

Her father cleared his throat, and in response, she looked down at her plate, knowing he would chastise her later. Father disapproved of the way the Earl of Hooke treated the son of a former mistress. While George Southwick wanted the union between Sebastian and Eliza, he didn't want his daughter to forget that her station was well above that of the illegitimate half-brother. Adam Faulkner did not deserve her attention or even her courtesy, as far as her father was concerned.

"Eliza," Amanda said, then added quickly, "Is it all right if I call you Eliza?"

"Of course."

"And you must call me Amanda. My brother tells me he introduced you to Countess this afternoon. Isn't she magnificent? She will produce many fine foals for the manor."

"Yes. Without a doubt."

"You know what I want?" Amanda didn't wait for a response. "I want to see the American mustangs and those spotted Indian ponies. I want to see them in person in their native elements. Not in photographs or in some show."

Eliza's eyes widened.

Amanda laughed. "When I was a girl, I saw some of them in Buffalo Bill's show in London during Queen Victoria's Golden Jubilee, but that isn't the same as seeing them in the wild. Can you imagine what that would be like?"

"No," she answered. "I can't."

"It's my heart's desire to travel to America and see the frontier before it's gone. Sebastian longs for such a trip as well. We want to go together in the spring."

"The deuce, you say!" Eliza's father stared at Amanda with a horrified expression.

Amanda was not cowed by the look. Instead, she leaned toward him. "It's true, Lord George. My brother is determined to spend time in America before he marries, and I am equally determined to go with him. Neither of us shall wed until we've lived a little."

"I'll be dashed. It's the first I've heard of such nonsense."

Eliza sensed her father's temper rising and shrank back, lest he blame her for this startling information.

"But it isn't nonsense," Amanda countered. "Why is

visiting America different from touring the Continent? No one thinks visiting Paris or Rome or even Greece is nonsense. I know many who have gone to America. But they don't seem to go farther than New York or Chicago. My brother and I want to see the Wild West."

Eliza's father huffed, apparent disbelief leaving him speechless.

ADAM KNEW he'd let the conversation go on too long. Southwick appeared angry—no doubt surprised to learn the viscount wanted to travel before entering into marriage—and his daughter's coloring had turned ashen. Amanda, on the other hand, was gathering momentum and could, at any moment, launch into one of her women's suffrage tirades unless he put a stop to it.

"Lord George." Adam stood. "Shall we retire to the smoking room?"

Southwick huffed again but rose from his chair. Obviously a man of habit.

Adam shot his half-sister a look, letting her know he wasn't happy. Whatever awaited him in the smoking room wouldn't be pleasant. Eliza's father didn't like him to begin with. His disapproval could only increase in the time they would be alone together.

"Would you care for a glass of brandy?" he asked as they entered the room off the library. "Or perhaps some port?"

"Brandy," the older man replied in a curt tone.

Adam filled a glass with the dark liquor and took it to Southwick. Then he went to an opposite sofa and sat.

Southwick held up a cigar, and the butler stepped forward to light it for him before retreating to the other side of the room, seeming to fade into the draperies. It amazed Adam, the way men like Lord George accepted the service of others without a word of thanks. With scarcely any recognition of their existence at all.

Strange, the world of the aristocracy. The rules. The pretense. To Adam, it felt artificial and cold. He loved his half-brother and half-sister. He even loved his father, as much as he was allowed. He was thankful he hadn't been left to a life of poverty or the wretched existence of the workhouse. That could have been his fate.

But he didn't envy Sebastian either. Unless he counted the woman his brother was to marry.

He cleared his throat, trying to dislodge the thought, and said, "I understand one of your horses could be a favorite in the Grand National."

Southwick looked pained when he answered. "We have a sporting chance." A frown drew his brows together. "Are you a gambling man?" It sounded like an accusation.

"No, my lord. As much as I love horses and enjoy racing, I prefer to spend my money in other pursuits."

Southwick grunted as he put his cigar back in the corner of his mouth.

Adam looked at the clock on the mantle and wished for another emergency from the stables.

As if in answer, the door to the room opened and Amanda stepped into view. While pointing, she mouthed the words, *Drawing room.* Adam answered with a slight nod. Fortunately, Southwick's back was to the door, and he didn't notice the exchange.

Adam waited another minute before asking, "Shall we join the ladies?"

Southwick studied his cigar—barely smoked—and the half-empty glass of brandy on the nearby table, then grunted. "Fine." He put the cigar in the ashtray and rose.

Leading the way from the smoking room, Adam said a silent thanks for Amanda's summons. But he might have to strangle Sebastian for leaving him in this situation.

His mood brightened considerably when they entered the drawing room. His gaze fell upon Eliza, perched on a settee near the fireplace. Firelight danced in her dark hair, and when she looked his way, her smile brightened the room even more. If a commoner like Adam Faulkner could see how wonderful she was, how perfectly lovely, what was wrong with men of the peerage? Why hadn't one of them asked for her hand long ago?

"Come, sit with us," Amanda called to the two men. "We were just discussing Glenhaven, Eliza's stallion. Adam, did you know he's a great-grandson of The Colonel?"

As Adam settled onto a chair, his gaze returned to Eliza. "No, I didn't know. The Colonel won the Grand National two years in a row. Quite an achievement."

"Yes." A pleased sparkle entered her eyes.

"When was that?"

"He won in 1869 and then again in 1870."

"Wasn't The Colonel taken to Germany?"

Eliza leaned forward. "Yes, but not before siring some foals in England. My grandfather bought one of those colts as a young man and that colt sired the mare, Biscuit, that my mother gave me the year before she died. Biscuit was Glenhaven's dam." She sat back, the pleasure fading from her eyes.

Adam understood. There was a sting whenever he thought of his own mother's passing. He had only the wisp of a memory of Caroline Faulkner. He recalled a bright summer day, the sky a clear blue, and the trees clothed in green leaves. Four years old, he'd hidden in some shrubs while she called and searched for him. She must have known where he was because he remembered her smile. He'd jumped from the bushes, giggling, and she grabbed him in her arms and whirled him around, her laughter joining his.

Looking at Eliza now, he wished he could ask her to share memories of her own mother. But before he could phrase the question, he was interrupted by her father.

"I understand you're expecting a rather large house party," Southwick said to Amanda.

"Yes, indeed. The manor will be quite full a few days from now. We asked you and your daughter to come early. I believe you and Father have something to discuss." She gave Eliza a meaningful glance before adding, "Others will begin arriving on Friday and even more on Monday."

Southwick gave another of his grunts.

Adam was beginning to seriously dislike that sound.

He looked in Eliza's direction again. Instead of sad, now she looked miserable. Could it have anything to do with the impending engagement?

Odd, how that question seemed to spark hope in his heart.

Chapter Four

While Adam watched from the center of the arena, a stable boy loped the bay mare in a wide circle. Countess might be the pride and joy of the Hooke stables, at least in the earl's estimation, but Adam was partial to this pretty lady. Her lines. The way she moved. Come spring, he would breed her, and if he could arrange it, the stud would be Glenhaven. Of course, making that happen would be easier if Eliza Southwick came to live at Hooke Manor as Sebastian's bride.

How was it possible to want something and not want it at the same time?

"Another beauty."

He turned as the subject of his thoughts walked toward him. Her dark hair was hidden beneath the hood of her cloak, and her cheeks were pink from her walk to the stables in the cold morning air.

"What's her name?" Eliza asked as she pushed back the hood.

"Miss Dorset."

"Is that where she comes from? Dorset."

"No, she was born on this estate. Amanda named her Miss Dorset because of something she read in a novel, but I never asked which one."

"And where is the sire?"

Adam motioned for the boy to ride the mare over to where he stood. "Owned by Sir John Carlisle of Carlisle Downs."

"Creed is the sire?"

It didn't surprise him that Eliza knew of the Carlisle stallion. He'd heard that George Southwick had tried to buy the horse on more than one occasion in recent years. But Sir John wasn't about to sell, and Adam didn't blame him.

Eliza stroked the mare's head. "I can see her sire in her."

"I think so too."

She turned her eyes in his direction. "You love working with the horses, don't you?"

"Yes, I do. But I like being with people as well. So many good folks on the estate and in the village."

"Do you manage the estate?"

"No. Only the stables. But I know many of the farmers, and I help as I can with matters pertaining to the tenants and other stock."

"Your fa— Lord Whitcombe must trust you a great deal."

So she knew the earl was his father. Not that it surprised him. His parentage had become an open secret long ago. Yet for some reason he'd wondered if

George Southwick had protected his daughter from that fact. Not that it should matter. She was intended for his half-brother, not him. Still, she knew the truth, and she continued to look at him with respect and—dare he believe—interest?

If she weren't a lady and he weren't misbegotten, he would have stepped close and stolen a kiss. Maybe he would have—

The sounds of an arriving carriage kept him from making a grave mistake. "That must be Lord Whitcombe and Sebastian."

Eliza turned to Miss Dorset and, eyes closed, pressed her forehead against the mare's forehead.

Was it possible she didn't *want* to marry his half-brother? And if she didn't—

"His lordship has returned," one of the stablehands called to Adam from the doorway.

"Thank you, Jenkins." He looked at the boy atop the mare. "Put her away for me, will you, Tom?"

"Yes, sir."

"Give her a good rubdown."

"I will, sir."

"Miss Southwick, shall we return to the house?"

Eliza gave one last stroke of the horse's head. "Yes. I suppose we shall." She faced him again while pulling her hood back over her hair.

He'd give anything to make her smile, the way she had when she'd entered the arena and seen Miss Dorset. If only he could.

Eliza was the last to enter the drawing room. Sebastian and Amanda, along with their father and hers, were already seated near the south facing windows, sunlight gilding the green and gold wall coverings and furniture.

Her father stood. "Ah, here she is. At last."

She forced a demure smile as she drew closer to the group. "Good morning, Father."

"Lord Whitcombe, Lord Sebastian, you remember my daughter."

The earl gave a nod.

Sebastian said, "It's good to see you again, Miss Southwick."

"And you, my lord."

"My sister tells me you've acquainted yourself with our stables since your arrival."

She felt warmth rise in her cheeks. "I have. I hope that's all right. You have some wonderful horses in your stables."

"Adam deserves the credit for that."

Her smile was more genuine now. "I thought as much."

Sebastian motioned to a set of chairs some distance from the others, inviting her to be seated. She obliged, and he sat beside her.

Keeping his voice low, he said, "I believe your interest in horses matches Adam's."

"I derive a great deal of enjoyment from working with horses." She glanced across the room. "My father doesn't approve of how much time I spend in our stables. He believes I should be more involved in…more feminine pursuits."

He leaned closer. "And my father would like to see his children follow his directives to the letter. But we often don't." He chuckled.

Sebastian Whitcombe was handsome, charming, and friendly, but Eliza saw in his eyes that he didn't want to make her his wife. Somehow she also knew that it wasn't personal. He wasn't rejecting her. He was rejecting marriage. She wanted to feel relief, but there were two older men in the room who wanted a union between their children. Who would win? Could Sebastian stand up to the earl? She couldn't refuse her father. George Southwick's daughter wasn't allowed a choice. Father would prefer it if she had no thoughts of her own, let alone speak them aloud.

She wished she could run from this room and go back to the stables. Rather than look into Sebastian Whitcombe's eyes, kind though they were, she would prefer to press her forehead against Miss Dorset's head and breathe in the mare's horsey scent. Or perhaps what she wanted was to look into Adam Faulkner's eyes. Eyes that were similar to his half-brother's but warmer, richer, more understanding, more—

"Miss Southwick?"

She blinked away the image in her mind and found herself still seated in the drawing room. "I'm sorry, Lord Sebastian. What did you say?"

A smile tweaked the corners of his mouth. "You would like to be elsewhere, wouldn't you?"

"You have no idea how much, my lord."

"Then let's go." He rose.

She glanced toward her father, but he was engrossed

in conversation with the earl. She stood and took Sebastian's proffered arm. Casually, the two of them walked to the far end of the room.

Eliza laughed as the door clicked closed behind them, feeling her heart lighten. "Do you think they even know we left?"

"I am not sure, but I suggest we not linger in the hall. Where would you like to go?" He held up a hand. "Wait. I know. The stables."

Had she misjudged this man? He seemed to know her well. He seemed to like her. Perhaps he wasn't averse to the marriage contract desired by their fathers.

"Would you like to ride?" he asked. "It's cold, but the sky is clear."

Her heart quickened with excitement. "I would love to ride."

"Then go change into your riding attire, Miss Southwick, and I will meet you at the stables."

She hesitated only a moment before spinning on her heel and hurrying toward the staircase. When she entered the bedchamber a few minutes later, her maid was there to greet her.

"I'm going riding, Mary."

The girl smiled brightly. "That's wonderful, miss." She went to the wardrobe and drew out Eliza's velvet riding habit.

"Hurry, Mary. I don't want to keep him waiting."

"The viscount, miss?"

She opened her mouth, ready to say yes, but then she realized it wasn't Sebastian she didn't want to keep waiting. There was another man she wanted to see.

Someone she hoped would be in the stables when she got there. Rather than prevaricate, she turned without replying and allowed her maid to help her out of her dress.

Twenty minutes later, Mary led the way to a back stairway. "There you go, miss," she said when they reached a rear entrance. "Have a good ride."

"I'm sure I will, Mary. Thank you." Eliza lifted her skirts and hurried toward the stables, feeling happier with every step.

Chapter Five

I offered to take Miss Southwick riding." Sebastian paced in front of a row of stalls. "But after some reflection, I fear it will give Father the wrong impression. I want you to take her in my stead. The poor girl is miserable. It should get better when our other guests start arriving, but for now she would do well to get some fresh air away from Lord George and Father."

Opposing emotions warred inside Adam's chest as he regarded his half-brother. He would love nothing better than to spend an hour or two on horseback with Eliza Southwick. But her father wouldn't approve and neither would his. Eliza was a lady. Adam was the Earl of Hooke's by-blow, the son who never should have been born. He wasn't a marriage prospect for someone like Eliza, no matter how much he liked her. If he cared for her reputation, he needed to remember his place. It would be best if he stayed out of sight until the house party was over.

"I shouldn't," he answered at last. "I have work to do."

"You take her riding, and I'll have another chat with Father. I must make him see reason. Despite what he thinks, I have plenty of time to marry and raise an heir."

"Miss Southwick is an amazing young woman, Sebastian. You could be making a mistake not to consider her."

His half-brother stopped pacing and gave Adam a hard look. "Amazing? Is she really?"

"If you'd spend a little more time with her, you would see that for yourself."

A smile flickered across Sebastian's face. "Is that right?"

"Yes. That's right." Adam spun on his heel and went to retrieve a sidesaddle from the tack room. When he returned, Eliza had entered the stables and stood near Sebastian. He overheard his half-brother say he couldn't ride with her after all.

"But I've asked Mr. Faulkner to accompany you," Sebastian added. "I wouldn't want you riding out alone."

"Oh...I..." She glanced toward Adam. "That's very kind of you, Mr. Faulkner."

"Not at all." His answer had come before he could stop himself.

This was a huge mistake. The earl wouldn't approve. Lord George wouldn't approve. No one would approve, with the possible exception of Sebastian and Amanda. On the Whitcombe estate, Adam was treated with kindness. Almost as an equal to his half-siblings. Almost as a real gentleman. But beyond Hooke Manor, he would forever be judged by his tarnished beginnings. He was illegitimate, and the gentry could never forgive him for that. Society didn't think it so terrible that the earl had had an affair with a young woman in the village all those years ago. He was a man, after all. He'd been a young and reckless one. And the woman was inconsequential. A village girl. But that a child had been born from the relationship and had the nerve to survive—that society abhorred.

Adam clenched his jaw. It wasn't often he contemplated the unfairness of being judged for his parents' choices, but—

Sebastian gave a slight bow to Eliza. "I will see you this evening at dinner, Miss Southwick." With a jaunty wave in Adam's direction, he strode away.

Eliza smiled at Adam, and that smile seemed to chase the shadows into hiding. It also chased away the tension that had tightened his shoulders only moments before.

By heaven, it was only a horseback ride. He was the stable manager. What difference if it was him or a stablehand or one of the footmen who accompanied her? She needed an escort. So he would be her escort. That was all his half-brother had asked him to do. A small favor.

With the assistance of young Tom, Adam had the two mounts bridled and saddled in no time at all, and soon thereafter, he and Eliza rode out of the stables in the direction of the woods that separated the manor house from the rest of the estate. Neither of them spoke as they continued at a sedate pace. Eliza looked about, her eyes taking in the wintery appearance of the land— the grass that had lost its green, the trees that had lost their leaves. Her expression was grave. Did she hope to become mistress here? Would she like to go riding daily in this park?

The road they followed entered the woods, and an instant later, Eliza's grave expression vanished, replaced by a smile as she urged her horse into a trot. Adam pressed his heels to the gelding's sides to catch up with her, but her mount was loping by then.

"Miss Southwick!"

Her laughter carried back to him on the crisp breeze.

Adam was of the opinion that riding sidesaddle took more skill than riding astride, and Eliza didn't disabuse him of that notion. The way she sat that mare. Horse and rider appeared to be one entity, moving smoothly and easily together. And when he caught up to them, he felt the joy emanating from the woman in the saddle. Being on horseback had transformed her. She'd never looked as pretty as she did at this moment.

Sebastian was insane not to want to claim this creature for his own. Adam would if he could. But he couldn't. It was an impossible desire.

Eliza glanced at him. Her eyes widened, and she drew back on the reins. Adam did the same.

"What's wrong?" she asked as soon as the horses had slowed to a walk.

"Wrong?" He cocked a brow. "Why would you think something was wrong?"

"You were glowering at me."

"Sorry. Must have been the sun in my eyes."

If she believed that, she was a fool. The morning sun was at their backs. But what else could he say? He didn't want to share the actual cause of his frown.

After a lengthy silence, Eliza asked, "Where will this road take us?"

He almost told her about the ruins of the old tower, a place he considered his private sanctuary. The desire to share it with her was strong. If they followed this road long enough, it would take them there. A tug in his heart told him that she would feel the same peace he found whenever he went there.

But in the end, he answered, "To the tenant farms. They make up the bulk of the estate."

"How many tenants are there?" There was genuine interest in her voice and in the gaze she turned on him.

He answered her question—and the half-a-dozen others that followed. Questions about the land, about the crops, about the people who lived and worked on the estate. Were other ladies of her class interested in such things? None that he'd run across. Granted, his experience with young women of quality was limited. Most noblemen didn't want their daughters sullied by his presence.

"You are not a mistake. You are precious in God's sight."

He hadn't remembered Lady Whitcombe's whispered words from his childhood in a long, long time. Strange that they should return to him now.

ELIZA SAW the frown return to Adam's face and knew he'd become lost in his own thoughts. Not that she blamed him. They hadn't been carrying on a scintillating conversation. At least, he probably hadn't thought so. She'd peppered him with questions, one after another, about the estate and what they were seeing, and she'd found his answers interesting. That he loved this place was evident. That he loved the people on the land was even more clear. That he was by far the most appealing man she'd ever met was undeniable.

"Mr. Faulkner, sir!"

At the sound of his name, Adam reined in his mount. Eliza did the same, then watched as a man about her father's age hurried toward them across the field to their right. He wore a loose-fitted sack coat— certainly not heavy enough to protect against the cold morning air—and as he drew closer, he removed his hat and held the brim before his chest with both hands.

"Mr. Faulkner, I thought you should know, sir. It's Mr. Cooper. He's had an accident."

"What happened, Moore?"

"He was repairing his roof, sir, and he fell off the ladder. I'm afraid he broke his leg."

"Has the doctor been to see him?"

"Cooper's saying he don't need a doctor. He's saying it's a waste of money that is scarce enough to come by."

Concern flooded Adam's face. "Go for the doctor, Moore. I'll see to the expense."

"Yes, Mr. Faulkner. I'll do it now."

After the man had gone on his way, Adam looked at

Eliza. "I'm afraid we must cut this ride short. I'm needed elsewhere."

"Are you going to Mr. Cooper's home?"

"After I see you back to the stables."

"There's no need to see me back. I'll go with you. Perhaps there is something I can do to help?"

"Miss Southwick, I—"

"Lead the way, Mr. Faulkner. I am quite determined to go with you."

"Lord George would not approve."

"My father doesn't approve of many things." She tilted her chin in a show of defiance and was immediately surprised by her own actions. She rarely defied her father—or anyone else. In truth, she had never defied her father in her life. Yet she did not want to be sent back to the manor. She wanted to render aid if possible. And if that meant going against her father's will, so be it.

Adam hesitated only a second before giving her a clipped nod. "Follow me." He nudged the gelding into a quick trot, not looking behind to see if she kept up.

Keeping up wasn't difficult. The mare she rode seemed prepared to do more than follow Adam's mount. The horse wanted to pull even and perhaps pass the gelding. Wisely, Eliza kept a firm rein, allowing Adam to lead the way.

Their destination was a small cottage with a tiled roof. A ladder leaned against the side of the house near the back corner. Although winter had made the yard look plain and gray, she saw signs of flower bushes that must make it colorful and lovely in the summer months.

Eliza might be ignorant of the management of a great estate, but she did know a farmer's wife had many other things to do to care for her family. There would be little time left for growing flowers. And yet it seemed the woman of this house managed it.

Adam dismounted and tied his gelding to a post before walking over to assist Eliza to the ground. When his hands took hold of her waist, a shock traveled through her. She sucked in a breath of air as she floated to the ground. She feared her legs might not support her when he let go, but they did. Barely.

Adam went to the door and knocked. Only moments passed before it opened, revealing a woman wearing a white cap on her head and an apron over a brown dress. Her face was careworn.

"Mr. Faulkner?" Her eyes widened.

"Mrs. Cooper, I heard of your husband's accident. I have come to see if there is anything I can do."

The woman shook her head. "Sir, I—"

"May I see him?"

This time she nodded, then opened the door wide.

Adam glanced over his shoulder at Eliza, inviting her with his look to follow him inside. The interior of the home smelled of woodsmoke and onion and cooking fats. Not that it was unclean. It wasn't. But the walls and furniture seemed to have soaked in years of cooking odors. The cottage had two rooms, the one at the back closed off with a curtain rather than a door.

As he closed the door, Adam said, "Eliza, I'd like you to meet Mrs. Cooper. Mrs. Cooper, this is Miss Eliza Southwick."

"I'm pleased to meet you, Miss Southwick," Mrs. Cooper said, ending with a small curtsey.

"If you'll both excuse me." Adam strode to the back room and moved beyond the curtain.

"Would you be wanting a cup of tea, miss?"

Eliza turned her gaze upon the woman and offered a slight smile. "That would be lovely, Mrs. Cooper. Thank you."

Mrs. Cooper hurried to the stove where she readied a kettle. While the water heated, she took two cups from a narrow shelf and placed them on the counter. "Please, sit yourself down, Miss Southwick." She looked over her shoulder at Eliza. "Best use the chair on the end of the table. The other's got an uneven leg. My Robby, he's always meaning to fix it but hasn't got around to it."

Eliza sat on the indicated chair. Cold air swirled around her, and a glance at the nearby window told her why. There were gaps between the frame and the wall. The front door of the cottage wasn't well-fitted either. Daylight—and the cold—streamed through in several places.

"It's kind of Mr. Faulkner to come see my husband."

"He's a kind man," Eliza agreed.

Mrs. Cooper smiled. "You know that about him, too. I'm glad. He is good."

Eliza looked in the direction of the back room. She heard Adam's voice from beyond the curtain, although it was too low for her to make out the words. She pictured him leaning over the bed to speak to the injured man. His expression would be filled with concern.

Adam is kind.

She lifted her eyes toward the ceiling where she saw watermarks in various places. The roof surely needed repairs.

Her gaze returned to Mrs. Cooper. "Is there…may I be of any assistance?"

"Oh, heavens no, miss. There is nothing to making a cup of tea."

Eliza hadn't meant the tea, but she didn't say so aloud. Still, she would think on the matter. There must be something she could do to help the Coopers. Or to help Adam help them.

Chapter Six

Anger emanated from Adam as he and Eliza rode back toward the manor house well over an hour later. She saw it in the furrow on his forehead and in the set of his shoulders. She simply didn't understand why he was angry.

"Are Mr. Cooper's injuries that bad?" she asked when she couldn't hold back the question any longer.

He looked at her, but it seemed to take several moments before he actually saw her. The frown disappeared as he shook his head. "Bad enough, but the doctor believes the leg will mend right."

"Then that is good."

"Yes." More of the tension left his shoulders. "It's the condition of the cottage that upsets me. Not just the Cooper cottage. Others on the estate as well. Repairs should be done, and it isn't the tenants who should have to make them."

"Have you said as much to the earl?"

He raised an eyebrow at her. "It isn't my place. I manage the stables. Not the estate."

"Mr. Faulkner, pardon me if I am speaking out of turn, but it seems to me that you should speak your mind. If you believe the tenants are being treated unfairly, who would be better than you to advise Lord Whitcombe of the state of affairs?"

"I doubt Mr. Bennett would agree with you." His expression darkened once again.

"Mr. Bennett?"

"The estate manager."

"And where was he when Mr. Cooper injured himself?"

"I have no idea."

She wondered if that was the truth. And perhaps she would have inquired further, but at that moment, the road they followed spilled out of the woods and the Hooke stables and manor house came into view. To her dismay, her father stood outside the stable entrance, arms crossed over his chest. She could feel his displeasure from where she sat on her horse. A blistering lecture was coming, the instant she was alone with him.

"Mr. Faulkner?" Eliza said softly.

"Yes."

"I am sorry for whatever my father may say to you once we reach the barn. Please know that I have enjoyed this morning far more than I can say. And if I don't have a chance to tell you later, I'm very grateful for the assistance you gave and will continue to give to Mr. and Mrs. Cooper. You are a generous man, Mr. Faulkner, with a good heart. I'm very happy to know you."

She nudged the mare into a faster walk, preferring to get her father's lecture over with as soon as possible.

How was a man supposed to respond to a comment like that?

Adam hurried to catch up with Eliza, but from the way she sat her horse—the rigid set of her shoulders and the tilt of her chin—as they approached Lord George, he decided it was not the time to respond. But if he could shield her from her father's anger he would.

He wasn't given the chance. The two riders were scarcely inside the stables before Eliza unhooked her right leg and half-jumped, half-slid from the sidesaddle. At once her father took hold of her left arm and propelled her in the direction of the manor. The silence between them seemed louder than if there'd been shouting. Would her father harm her? If that man—

Sebastian stepped from the shadows. "You were gone longer than I expected."

Adam gave his half-brother a hard look before dismounting. At the same time, the stable boy came out of the tack room and, without instructions, led the mare toward her stall.

Sebastian cleared his throat. "I believe Lord George would like to depart for Briar Park this afternoon and forego the festivities. But he won't. He'll see reason."

Adam stroked the gelding's neck.

"There won't be any announcement of an engagement to Miss Southwick. Not this week. Not ever."

This drew Adam's gaze.

"I made it clear to Father that, while Miss Southwick is a lovely young woman, I am not ready for that commitment. Father, in turn, has made my position clear to Lord George."

"That must have been some conversation." Adam removed the gelding's saddle. "And what are the consequences of your decision?"

"Unknown. I know I will have to marry, but I can't think about that yet. I'm determined to have my time in America first."

Adam faced his half-brother again. "America? You're actually going?"

Sebastian beamed. "I am. I have an American friend. We went to school together. He's offered a place for me to stay. A cattle ranch in the west. Roger Bernhardt is coming along. And Amanda will persuade Father to agree for her to go, too. Never underestimate her. Why don't you join us?"

"I haven't the funds, for one reason. For another, I have obligations on the estate."

"Father could find another stable manager to fill in while you're gone."

Adam didn't want to admit, even to himself, that was what he feared. He could be replaced. He picked up a brush and began grooming the horse.

Sebastian appeared on the opposite side of the gelding. "Would you like to know another reason I am not interested in Miss Southwick?" He crossed his arms atop the horse's broad back.

Adam grunted.

"Because there is another man who has drawn her interest, and I would never want to be second choice for the woman I marry."

"I never thought you the type to listen to gossip." Adam stopped brushing to meet Sebastian's gaze.

"It isn't gossip. I've seen it for myself."

"When have you seen this man of interest? You told me that your path hasn't crossed Eliza's in a long while."

"Adam, old fellow, you are obtuse." With that, Sebastian left the barn.

Obtuse? Name-calling seemed unnecessary. Adam glanced at Tom who had removed the saddle from Eliza's mount and was now brushing the mare with unhurried strokes. If the boy had been listening to the two men, he gave no sign of it. And it wasn't likely the lad would have known the meaning of the word. Obtuse? Was he really slow to understand? And about what?

A cold shiver ran through him. Whether he was obtuse didn't matter. Was it true that Eliza cared for another man? Was her heart already taken? Who was this man and why hadn't Southwick pursued an arrangement with him instead of Sebastian? Maybe he was unsuitable. Or maybe he was engaged to another.

The last thought was like a punch in the gut. After all, he knew more than a little about wanting something —or someone—he couldn't have.

Chapter Seven

M ore guests began arriving before noon on Friday. Eliza was glad to see them come. Her father had been in such a foul temper for the past two days. Only the chance that she might draw the interest of another eligible guest of the Earl of Hooke had kept her father from bolting after learning that Viscount Willowthorpe had refused to enter into a marriage contract with his daughter.

All Eliza felt was relief. This was a reprieve. It wouldn't last. She knew that well enough. But for the remainder of their stay, she intended to enjoy herself. She wouldn't be under pressure to be winsome or fascinating or coy whenever Sebastian Whitcombe was around. She could be herself.

The first guests to arrive were Lord Christopher Mersey and his sister Lady Charlotte. They were soon followed by three carriages carrying a half dozen young men, ranging in ages from perhaps twenty-two to thirty-five, and five females, all of them close to Amanda's age. They had come up from London on the train.

That this was a house party for young people was apparent. Eliza's father would be pleased with some of the prospects, too. There were two future earls and one future marquis in the mix.

As for Eliza, she would rather be in the barn with Adam. She hadn't seen him since their ride two days earlier, and she missed his company. She wondered how Mr. Cooper was faring and whether Adam had talked to Lord Whitcombe about the condition of the tenant cottages. She wondered—

"Miss Southwick," Amanda's voice intruded. "A number of us plan to go riding this afternoon. You'll want to join us, I'm sure."

Her heart lifted. "I would love to." She would see Adam. Surely she would see him when they all went to the stables.

Amanda drew her toward some of the other young ladies, pulling her into the conversation. Several complained about the first class coach on the train. Very substandard. Another bemoaned how dreary London was at present and how eager she was for the first ball of the season. There was a great deal of laughter and more than a few glances cast in the direction of the gentlemen who were conversing on the opposite side of the room.

Eliza had never excelled at flirtation. Perhaps she was too honest and plain-spoken for it—with everyone but her father. She supposed her honesty was one reason she had remained unattached in her first seasons while other young ladies of her age and class made matches.

She didn't know how to pretend interest or attraction when there wasn't any. It wasn't that gentlemen—or ladies—disliked her. They simply liked others more than they liked her.

Just as she liked Adam Faulkner more than she liked anyone else.

She sucked in a breath at the thought. It wasn't that liking him was a surprise. She'd liked him from the night they first met in the Briar Park stables. But this was different. This went deeper. She wanted something… more…with Adam.

Something she couldn't have.

Or could she?

The question seemed to repeat in her mind, over and over, and with it came anxiety as her maid helped her into her riding habit that afternoon. The anxiety increased as she and the other ladies and men made their way to the large barn where their mounts awaited them. When she passed through the open stable doors, she saw more than a dozen horses saddled and ready. But she didn't see Adam. Disappointment sluiced through her.

Mild chaos reigned inside the barn as men and women mounted their horses. Laughter rose to the rafters as the party walked their horses outside before following the same road that Adam and Eliza had taken two days earlier. They hadn't traveled far before the riders fell into sets of two. Lord Mersey wound up beside Eliza.

"You look lovely today, Miss Southwick," he said, feigned charm in his voice.

Even when she was seventeen, she wouldn't have been drawn to Christopher Mersey. Oh, he was handsome, but he was even more aware of his own good looks than she was.

He smiled as he studied her. "I didn't see you at the Chesterton Ball."

"We weren't in town at the time. The season was winding down, and Father was eager to return to Briar Park."

"That's a shame. It was a wonderful affair. But it always is."

"Yes. It always is."

What she wanted to say was that all balls and other gatherings during the London Season blended together in her memory. The conversations were the same. The music was the same. Even the people were very much the same. If one was missing, someone else stepped into their place and said the same insipid words. Come to think of it, it surprised her that Lord Mersey had realized her absence.

Across the field on her right, she saw the Cooper cottage. A wagon with a team of horses stood close to one side of the house. Nearby was a saddle horse, grazing. Movement drew her gaze to the roof where two men worked.

Adam.

She knew it was him, even from a distance. She couldn't see him clearly but she knew, and her heart performed acrobatics in her chest. Eliza was so intent on the cottage in the distance that she hadn't noticed Amanda falling back to ride on her left side.

"Christopher," Amanda said, "why don't you see if you can help solve a disagreement between my brother and Lord Hendricks? Something to do with cards or gambling." She flicked her fingers, urging him away.

"As you wish, Lady Amanda." He kicked his mount into action.

"He can be rather a bore," Amanda said softly as soon as Lord Mersey was out of earshot.

Eliza laughed. "Yes. But it wasn't his fault this time. I was distracted."

"I could tell." Amanda looked across the field. "Adam had a long talk with Sebastian yesterday. It seems our estate manager has not been keeping up with things the way he should. Adam knew it but Sebastian didn't. Would you care to see the work they're doing on that cottage?"

Her eyes widened. "I don't imagine they want a party of riders mulling about the yard."

"I didn't mean all of us. We'll let the others ride on. You and I can go on our own."

WHEN ADAM NOTICED the large group of riders on the road from the manor, he shaded his eyes, searching for Eliza among them. He hoped her disappointment about Sebastian—surely she *was* disappointed—had been eased by the company of others of her class. He hoped she was able to laugh and enjoy herself. He wanted her to be happy. If not with his half-brother, then with someone else. Someone worthy of her.

Why did that thought feel like a lie?

Two horses, each one carrying a woman, broke away from the back of the group. They cantered across the fallow field toward the cottage. As the pair drew closer, he recognized his half-sister's mount. Then one of the riders laughed. Eliza. He would know her laughter anywhere. For the last few nights, he'd heard it in his dreams.

Amanda's voice floated to him on the breeze. "That doesn't look like easy work." She reined in her horse near the cottage, shielding her eyes against the sunlight spilling through the gray cloud cover.

"It isn't." He straightened. "I see the rest of the house party has arrived."

"Apart from a couple of Father's friends, yes. Everyone is here. You should join us tonight for supper."

A scoff escaped him.

Amanda drew her mount to a halt and stared up at him with an impudent look. "Why not?"

"Because I haven't been invited."

"I'm inviting you."

"Amanda." He drew out her name slowly.

"Adam." She drew his out in the same way.

Unable to keep himself from it, he glanced at Eliza. The way she smiled back at him made him almost dizzy. If he wasn't careful, he'd wind up falling off the roof and breaking his leg like Cooper.

"Mr. Faulkner," Eliza said, "I would like it if you came. Perhaps Lady Amanda will arrange it so you can sit next to me." Her cheeks turned a lovely pink that had nothing to do with the cold, and she lowered her eyes.

"Lord George wouldn't like it, even if you would."

Her gaze snapped up again. "This isn't his home. It isn't his choice."

And I'm not his choice either. Could she read that thought in his eyes?

"Don't be a bore, Adam," Amanda said. "You are not a stranger to the dining room at Hooke Manor nor are you a stranger to some of our guests."

First he was obtuse. Now he was a bore. When had he become a target for sibling abuse?

"Amanda." He didn't draw the name out this time, but he made his exasperation clear in his tone.

"Good. We dine at eight. Don't be late."

With a wave, Amanda turned her horse away. Eliza kept her gaze on Adam a few moments longer before she followed after his half-sister.

"You could never have won, Mr. Faulkner."

He looked at Donald Shaw, the tenant farmer who'd volunteered to help Adam with the roof repair. "No, Shaw. I think you're right about that. I've never been able to resist Lady Amanda's wishes, even when she was a little girl."

"*Especially* when they're little girls," Shaw said with a shake of his head. "Most of us are putty in their hands. I know it's true with my wee daughter."

"Indeed." Adam bent to return to his work, but it wasn't his half-sister's face and voice that lingered in his memory, and he wasn't going to the supper party because of Amanda's persuasion either.

Chapter Eight

Adam straightened the white evening tie as he stood before the mirror in the bedroom of his cottage. He'd worn this same black suit on the night Eliza and her father arrived, but now he found himself questioning if it was fine enough. Not that it had seen much use.

When Adam mingled with Sebastian's friends, it usually had something to do with horses. No suit was required in those situations. But he'd attended nice suppers and even the occasional soiree over the years. He knew what was required of him tonight.

He also knew that he could look like a gentleman, live like a gentleman, and even act like a gentleman. But he could never *be* a gentleman. Eliza deserved a gentleman. She deserved to live in a fine house with plenty of servants to see to her every want and desire. What was he thinking to want to marry a woman like her?

And he did want to marry her. Perhaps he didn't know her well enough to call his feelings love, but they would become love, with a little time and proximity. He was sure of it. As sure as he'd ever been about anything. He'd known it that first night in the Briar Park stables, and all this time later, he knew it still.

Drawing a breath, he turned away from the mirror.

The walk to the manor house wasn't far, but the evening had turned bitter cold. He hunched his shoulders and leaned into the wind.

Southwick had wanted his daughter to marry the future Earl of Hooke. Adam would inherit no title. If Eliza chose him for a husband, she would have to give up everything familiar. She would likely have to give up seeing her father and her younger brother, too. She wouldn't be invited to balls or private teas with countesses or duchesses. Mr. and Mrs. Faulkner wouldn't go to London for the season. Some of her old friends would be polite but distant. Others would give her the cut direct. Could he ask that of her?

He remembered the way she looked at him whenever they were together. Did she like him well enough to leave her own world for his?

"God, I must be insane to harbor such thoughts." He glanced at the heavens, the stars hidden behind clouds. "If this is the way You have for me and I should walk in it, make it clear. Don't let me ask it if asking will harm her."

Once inside the house, he paused, rubbed his hands together, and stomped his feet, all in an effort to get the blood moving again. Then he wended his way along corridors and hallways toward the drawing room. It wasn't long before he heard voices and laughter.

Although the sounds were happy ones, he wanted to turn and go in the other direction.

"Mr. Faulkner, I would like it if you came."

The memory of Eliza's words kept him moving forward.

When he first stepped into the drawing room, his presence went unnoticed. Guests and family mingled in groups, some seated on furniture, others standing near the fireplace. His gaze found Eliza alone near a window placed between two ceiling-to-floor bookcases. There was a slight slump to her shoulders, revealing a sadness he couldn't see in her face. He followed the direction she was looking and saw Lord George and Sebastian together in a far corner. Their voices weren't raised, but he knew his half-brother well enough to recognize controlled anger in the set of his jaw. And if he wasn't mistaken, others in the room had started to recognize it as well. Conversations began to fall silent, one by one by one.

"Adam!" Amanda's voice was filled with false cheer. "You're here at last. I told you not to be late."

He took a few steps deeper into the room as she approached him. "I'm not late."

Amanda slipped her arm through his. "Help me distract them," she whispered.

"Distract whom?"

"Anyone. Everyone." She affected her prettiest smile before she addressed Charlotte Mersey. "Lady Charlotte, do you know Mr. Faulkner?"

"No, I don't believe we've ever met." She gave him a slight nod.

He bowed in return. "A pleasure, Lady Charlotte."

The look in her eyes said she knew his relationship to Amanda. He suspected she was the sort who would want to put him in his place, should the opportunity arise.

Amanda tugged him toward some of the male guests, and he relaxed a little. He knew all of them, at least by sight. They exchanged greetings.

"And, of course, you remember our lovely Miss Southwick."

His heart gave a little hiccup as his gaze met with Eliza's. "Of course." He bowed. "Miss Southwick."

"Mr. Faulkner." A smile tugged at the corners of her mouth, and the sadness vanished from her eyes.

"Oh," Amanda said, innocence in her tone, "there's Wilson. Adam, will you escort Miss Southwick to the dining room." Then she was off to tell the rest of the party that supper was about to be served.

Now his pulse was pounding in his ears as he offered his arm to Eliza. "Shall we, Miss Southwick?"

"Yes." Her fingers pressed into the curve of his arm. "I believe we shall, Mr. Faulkner."

Was there more meaning behind her reply? Or did he simply wish there to be more?

———

Amanda had placed Adam beside Eliza at the supper table, just as Eliza had hoped. Even more ingenious, their hostess had given Lord George a seat on the same side of the table but at the opposite end, making it hard

—if not impossible—for Eliza's father to observe her during the meal.

God bless you, Amanda Whitcombe, she thought as she took her assigned chair.

With everyone settled, it was clear that Amanda had broken more than a few rules of convention in the seating arrangements. Rank hadn't influenced her in the least. But no one seemed to object. Even Eliza's father said nothing. Perhaps whatever Sebastian said to him earlier had silenced him for a time.

Servants came and went, offering a delightful selection of food. Eliza took a little of everything, although she doubted she would eat a bite. Not with Adam sitting so close beside her.

"Were you able to finish the repairs on that roof?" she asked when the opportunity came.

"Not completely. More needs to be done. But the Coopers will stay dry."

"I'm glad."

"I only wish I'd realized the conditions sooner."

"But it isn't your responsibility."

He looked surprised. "No. Not as a part of my job. But as a neighbor, I wish I'd known. The cottage I live in has been kept in excellent condition. Perhaps because it is in view of the house. But I should have noticed the others. I could have given Cooper help before he ended up injured."

His reply brought a feeling of warmth to her chest. Adam Faulkner might not be a gentleman by birth, but his caring, generous heart made him a prince among men as far as she was concerned.

"Perhaps," she said, "I could do something to ease Mrs. Cooper's worries while her husband is unable to work."

Now he looked amused. "What do you suppose that would be?"

She felt a sting of irritation. "I don't know. Perhaps I could provide some food for them."

"That would be exceedingly kind of you." He leaned closer, the amusement gone, and lowered his voice even more. "I could take you into the village to do the shopping."

"I would like that." She had never been inside a grocer's shop in her life. She wouldn't know a good potato from a bad one or how to select a choice cut of meat. She sometimes sent a request to the cook at Briar Park for a different main dish or for a delicious pastry, but that was as close as she'd come to deciding on a menu. Father thought such things were best left to the Briar Park cook. But none of that seemed to matter at the moment.

"You surprise me, Miss Southwick."

"I do?"

"Yes."

"Why?"

"I'm not sure I can explain it."

Try, she wanted to say.

"You are brave."

She drew slightly back. "You thought I was afraid."

"I thought…" He paused, then went on, "I thought you might yield more to convention."

"You would not be wrong, Mr. Faulkner." She

glanced in the direction of the earl at the far end of the table. He would have to do since she couldn't see her own father. "I don't often stand my ground. At times, I do what is easiest. I usually do the conventional thing."

"You would have married Sebastian to please your father." It wasn't a question.

She met Adam's gaze again. "I would have married him. But I'm glad I will not have to."

He smiled.

Her pulse fluttered.

"Don't misunderstand me, sir. I like Lord Sebastian. From what I know of him, he is a decent man. Other men respect him. *You* respect him. And I have seen him with his sister, and he is kind and patient with her. I would expect him to be the same with a wife. But I do not love him. I am not attracted to him." She felt heat rise in her cheeks and looked down at the barely-touched food on her plate.

"I, for one, am thankful for that, Miss Southwick."

She looked up again. Did he mean—? *Could* he mean—?

"Tomorrow," he said, "if the weather stays fair, we'll go into the village and fill several baskets with foodstuffs for the Coopers. Shall we say ten in the morning?"

Unable to speak for the emotions whirling inside her, Eliza nodded.

Chapter Nine

After successfully avoiding her father after supper on Friday evening, Eliza decided to skip breakfast rather than tempt fate. She waited in her bedchamber, checking the clock every five to ten minutes. It was barely half past nine when she could wait no longer. She slipped out of the room and made her way to the back of the house.

Only a few days before, she would have become lost in the labyrinth of hallways and narrow staircases. But not today. She moved with confidence and excitement because she was moving toward Adam Faulkner.

Was this love?

The question brought her to a halt before she reached the door.

Was this love?

Hand pressed against her stomach, she forced herself to take a deep breath, then another.

Be wise, Eliza. Be careful.

She wasn't a reckless woman. She preferred to think

on things before making a decision. But when she thought of Adam, common sense and patience seemed to flee.

Father was already angry that there would be no marriage contract with Lord Sebastian. Now he wanted her to entice one of the other gentlemen at this house party. One nobleman was almost the same as another, in her father's mind. He would marry her off to any man with the right pedigree and title. As Eliza had known when they set off from Briar Park, Father wasn't concerned about her happiness. He simply expected her obedience. And if she defied him—as she was defying him now—what would he do?

She glanced over her shoulder, looking back the way she'd come. Like Lot's wife, she thought. No, she mustn't look back. She couldn't settle for someone who wouldn't engage her mind and heart, especially since her heart was already full of another.

She moved to the door, opened it, and went outside. The day was gloomy, as was so often true of this time of the year, but the clouds didn't seem to threaten rain. Not yet. She pulled her cloak close about her and hurried to the stables. Inside the cavernous building, stable boys mucked stalls while grooms brushed horses and two more horses were being exercised. It seemed even busier inside the barn today than yesterday when almost all the Whitcombe guests went riding.

"Miss Southwick."

She turned at the sound of Adam speaking her name, her heart doing that wonderful-terrible skitter that happened so often around him. "Good morning, Mr. Faulkner."

He motioned to the rear exit. "I have a carriage waiting for us outside. It's larger than we require, but it will make it easier to deliver our purchases." He reached for her hand and tucked it into the crook of his arm.

His move seemed to lay claim to her. It was bold of him. And she found she liked it.

"Will you ride inside with me?" she asked as they approached the vehicle.

He smiled. "I can't drive the horses from inside."

"Of course not. But you could ask someone else to drive us."

"I could." His smile slipped a little. "But I think it is better, for now, that I drive instead."

There was that flutter again. "Why is that, Mr. Faulkner?"

A lengthy silence followed before he answered, "You need to be very certain you know what it is you want, Miss Southwick."

Don't look back, Eliza. Don't be Lot's wife. Be wise and careful, but don't look back.

After a moment, Adam released her arm and stepped away to open the carriage door. When he offered his hand, this time to help her into the vehicle, she took it without meeting his gaze. She couldn't look at him yet. Her emotions were too unsettled.

Eliza had ridden alone in a carriage many times, but never had she been so aware of the unseen driver seated outside and above her. She wished she could ride up on that seat next to him. But what a scandal that would cause. She imagined her father's cheeks all puffed out and red, and she laughed. Only she shouldn't laugh. Such a thing might kill him, and she didn't wish him dead. She only wanted to have happiness in her marriage. Which meant she wanted to have regard for her husband, to know tenderness and affection, if not love.

The laughter faded away.

In all her seasons, in all of the balls and soirees she'd attended, no one had made her feel the way Adam Faulkner did. She didn't know why. She only knew it was true.

IN THE LANE outside the baker's shop, Adam assisted Eliza from the carriage. He was chilled through from the drive into the village, but looking at her as she stepped to the ground warmed him again.

"Shall we start here?" He motioned to the bakery.

She nodded.

They went inside, and Eliza had soon purchased nearly every delicacy in the shop. The Coopers were used to simple loaves of bread. Cakes and pies and other sweet pastries were the stuff of rare celebrations. What would they think when Eliza delivered her purchases?

They would think how kind she was, he answered himself. How generous she was.

How perfect she was.

Eliza wasn't content until she and Adam had visited every shop in the small village, not including the carpentry shop and the blacksmith shop. Flour and sugar, beef and mutton, soon joined the pastries on the floor of the carriage, and before she was ready to make the delivery to the Cooper cottage, she bought some fabric, ribbon, and yarn saying, "I'm sure Mrs. Cooper would like a new dress or a new shawl."

Adam and Eliza were approaching the carriage for the final time when someone called his name. He stopped, causing Eliza to do the same. When he turned, he saw a man he knew well striding toward them.

"I saw the Whitcombe carriage," Roger Bernhardt said as he drew near. "Are you returning to Hooke Manor?"

Adam glanced at Eliza, and she gave the slightest of nods. Then Adam said, "Miss Southwick, may I introduce Roger Bernhardt."

Surprise flickered across Roger's face before he bowed to acknowledge the introduction. "An honor, Miss Southwick."

"Mr. Bernhardt is a good friend of Sebastian's," Adam added.

Eliza gave Roger a smile and a nod.

"Mr. Bernhardt is an artist. Have you noticed the portrait of the earl in the grand salon? He painted that."

"Truly, Mr. Bernhardt? I remember thinking how unusual for a portraitist to be completely honest about his subject."

"I'll take that as a compliment."

"I meant it as one."

Adam cupped Eliza's elbow with his hand. "Miss Southwick and I are delivering some supplies to one of the farmers on the estate before returning to the manor."

"May I ride along?" Roger asked. "I walked here from the train station."

"That's ten miles."

"I know, and I'd prefer not to have to walk the rest of the way."

"Of course you may come with us." He took a step closer to the carriage, drawing Eliza with him. "But why didn't you arrange to have someone meet you at the station? They would have sent a carriage for you."

"I did let Sebastian know when to expect me, but he must not have received my message in time."

Adam looked at Eliza again. "Then let's be on our way."

He liked Roger Bernhardt. The son of a successful London merchant, Roger was one of Sebastian's closest friends. Adam was able to consider the man a friend as well. But that didn't mean he liked the idea of him sitting in the carriage with Eliza while Adam rode in the driver's seat. The idea made his jaw clench, and it took only a moment to recognize it as jealousy. He didn't want to share her with another man. Not even in a way that society would approve.

But what choice did he have?

"I DIDN'T EXPECT to meet you like this, Miss Southwick," Roger Bernhardt said as the carriage jerked into motion.

"You were expecting to meet me?"

He looked confused. "Well, yes. Sebastian told me you and your father were coming to Hooke Manor for this house party. I know I'm a couple of days late, but I assumed you would still be here and we would be introduced."

Which meant Sebastian had also told his friend what his father—and hers—had hoped to accomplish this week. Mr. Bernhardt, no doubt, had expected to arrive to some kind of celebration. He'd expected Sebastian to go along with the earl's wishes.

Eliza kept her expression placid. "Many expectations have not been met this week."

Understanding dawned in his eyes. "Ahh."

Once again, she wished she was on the driver's seat next to Adam. Because what else could she have to say to this stranger.

"So no new stallion in the Hooke stables," Roger said. "The earl must be disappointed."

She felt her eyes widen.

"Miss Southwick, I do apologize." Embarrassment darkened his face. "I didn't mean that to sound the way it did."

Her surprise faded. "Did you speak anything but the truth? It's likely the earl is more upset about Glenhaven than losing me as a daughter-in-law."

"True or not, I should not have said it. I dishonored my friend by speaking so carelessly."

She drew a deep breath. "Mr. Bernhardt, I did not wish to marry Lord Sebastian, and he most surely did not want to marry me. While our fathers may not be happy, we are both content with the decision that was made."

"No doubt Lord Whitcombe would like to buy the stallion from you."

"Glenhaven is not for sale."

"Too bad. Adam is a genius with horses. He could transform the Hooke stables with a stud like yours."

Her gaze flicked in the direction of the driver's seat above Roger Bernhardt's head. Was Adam only showing interest in her because of her horse? Icy cold shivered through her at the thought. Was she that undesirable?

Tears stung her eyes, and a lump formed in her throat.

The drive to the Cooper cottage seemed to take forever.

Chapter Ten

Adam frowned as he slipped his right arm into his coat. Would Eliza join the Whitcombe family for church this morning? He hoped so. He wanted to see her. He *needed* to see her. The scowl deepened as he put his left arm into the remaining sleeve, then adjusted the coat while regarding his reflection in the mirror.

Eliza's mood had changed between their time in the village and their arrival at the Cooper cottage to deliver their purchases. She'd seemed happy when he helped her into the carriage. Had something happened during the drive? Had Roger warned her away from the likes of Adam Faulkner?

No, that didn't make sense. Roger had no reason to do that. He didn't think himself better than Adam. At least he'd never exhibited such feelings in their interactions. So what had gone wrong? Why had Eliza seemed withdrawn and unhappy when she'd bid him goodbye yesterday outside the stables?

The questions repeated over and over in his head as

he walked to the chapel on the Whitcombe estate. He'd only been a lad of four the first time he'd come to this small church, but the memory of it was fixed in his mind. Perhaps because Lady Whitcombe, the Countess of Hooke, had taken his hand and led him inside.

She'd been a kind and loving woman, the countess. No one in society would have blamed her if she'd ignored or rejected the son of her husband by another woman. He supposed it helped that she and the earl hadn't married until more than two years after Adam had been born. Had she even known of his existence before his mother died?

Another memory came to mind. The day Lady Whitcombe had been laid to rest. Five-year-old Amanda had been returned to the nursery by her nanny, and fifteen-year-old Sebastian had taken a horse from the stables and ridden off to be by himself. Adam—no longer a boy at the age of eighteen but feeling like a child—had come to the chapel to privately mourn the woman who had made his boyhood happy, for the most part. She'd made him feel acceptable in a world that didn't want to accept him. She'd shown him true Christian charity, and he'd loved her for it.

Adam had only one brief memory of his own mother. That and a grainy photograph, corners bent and edges cracked. But his memories were filled with images of Sebastian and Amanda's mother.

The chapel came into view, and his thoughts returned to the present. And to Miss Eliza Southwick.

Most of the guests of the Whitcombes had come to the church for worship this morning, filling many of the pews in the small sanctuary. The earl, Sebastian, and Amanda sat in their usual pew, and Adam took his place at the back of the church.

It didn't take long for him to find Eliza. Even with her back to him and her dark hair hidden beneath a large hat covered in feathers and other decorations, he knew her. Perhaps it was the set of her shoulders.

The vicar stepped to the podium. He opened with a reading from the Scriptures before bowing his head in prayer. "O God, whose blessed Son was manifested that He might subdue sin and death—" his voice boomed throughout the chapel, magnified by the stone walls "—and make us the sons of God, and heirs of eternal life; Grant us, we beseech thee, that, having this hope, we may purify ourselves, even as He is pure; that when He shall appear with power and great glory, we may be made like unto Him in His eternal kingdom, where He liveth, and in the unity of the Spirit with Thee, O Father; world without end. Amen."

Adam's thoughts centered on his Creator. "Amen," he whispered. And with no small effort, he mentally placed his feelings for Eliza and his desire for a life with her on the altar before God. He had not because he asked not, and so he asked.

ELIZA HADN'T SLEPT well the previous night, and weariness tugged at her eyelids as the vicar preached his sermon. Even more, despair tugged at her heart. The doubt that had begun in the carriage ride from the village to the cottage yesterday had seemed to double and then triple overnight as she'd tossed and turned.

"For as the Psalm tells us," the vicar said, "the steps of a good man are ordered by the Lord. God delighteth in his way. Though he fall, he shall not be utterly cast down. We know that the Lord upholdeth him with his hand."

My steps are ordered by God. The words seemed to vibrate through her, awakening her. *I can trust Him to lead me. He holds me by my hand.*

She closed her eyes, and the vicar's voice receded into the background while she prayed. She prayed as she hadn't prayed in a long time. She wouldn't give in to despair. She would trust and watch. She would follow the path before her. God wouldn't lead her astray. Her life might not be exactly as she wished it, but it would be exactly as God ordained.

Strange, how much brighter the chapel felt when she opened her eyes again.

A short while later, the vicar closed the service with another prayer, and people all around her began to rise and depart the chapel. Eliza remained in the pew. The sound of voices faded away until she was surrounded by silence.

God would guide her. God would hold her hand. But did that mean she must be passive?

She sat straighter. "I should ask Adam," she said softly.

"Ask me what?"

She gasped at the unexpected voice.

Hat in hand, Adam stepped into view in the far aisle,

drawing her gaze to him. "Ask me what, Miss Southwick?" His tone was gentle, almost a caress. Patience filled his expressive eyes.

"Why have you… Why have you been so…kind to me?"

"Kind?"

She shook her head. Kind wasn't the right word. It wasn't what she'd meant to say.

He sat on the pew. "May I ask you something first?"

Holding her breath, she nodded.

"What happened yesterday to make you sad?"

She answered with another question of her own. "You would like to have Glenhaven in the stables of Hooke Manor, wouldn't you?"

His brows drew together. "As stable manager, I would be a fool not to want such a horse. A great-grandson of The Colonel. We could breed him to our finest mares. What amazing offspring they would have. Perhaps future Grand National champions, not many years from now."

She stared down at her hands, folded in her lap. "And what would you do to get Glenhaven for the earl? To what lengths would you go?"

Silence filled the chapel once again. Silence except for the blood pounding in her ears.

"Is that what you think of me, Miss Southwick?"

She dared to look at him again, and the hurt on his face pierced her. "I don't… I didn't—" She broke off, not knowing how to answer. It *was* what she'd thought of him. At least for a short while. But now?

Adam set his hat on his head as he rose from the

pew. "I would do whatever is right and honorable to improve the Whitcombe stables. I pay fair prices for the horses I buy for the earl, and I negotiate with the intent of obtaining my goal. But I try to act with integrity in all of my business dealings and in all of my relationships." He cleared his throat. "I may not be a gentleman by birth, Miss Southwick. I cannot change that. But I try to behave as a gentleman in every other aspect of my life."

He turned on his heel and was gone before Eliza could form a reply.

She'd wounded him. She'd wanted to know what he felt for her, but instead, she'd accused him. Yesterday, careless words from Mr. Bernhardt had caused her to doubt and suspect, and now she'd passed along her hurt to Adam. The man who had shown her nothing but respect and…and something more.

"O God, I'm sorry," she whispered.

Chapter Eleven

E liza's father looked up from the newspaper in his hands when she entered the drawing room. "Where have you been? The others returned from the chapel nearly an hour ago."

"I went for a walk. I wanted to think."

"You think too much as it is. No man wants a bluestocking for a wife."

She went to the sofa opposite him. "Father, I'm not a bluestocking. But I would like to marry a man who likes *me* the way I am."

He looked down again. "Who would that be?"

His words hurt, but she pressed on. "What if I chose to marry someone without a title? What if I married someone without your blessing?"

Anger sparked in his eyes as he laid the newspaper aside. "I would disown you."

"Is it so terrible that I wish to marry for love and not for position?" Tears stung her eyes, and she blinked them back.

"I knew it was a waste of time to stay at Hooke Manor. You haven't the good sense to try to win the attention of a man like Lord Mersey. Even when he's in the same room with you. We should have returned to Briar Park once I knew there would be no marriage contract."

She stood. "No, it wasn't a waste of time to stay here." Head held high, she left the room. Blinded by her tears, she nearly ran into Amanda Whitcombe near the staircase.

"Eliza, what is it?"

She sniffed. "Nothing."

"Someone has upset you."

Eliza shook her head.

"You may as well tell me." Amanda hooked arms with Eliza and drew her into an empty room. "I won't be put off. We are friends. We were almost family." She put a hand over her mouth, then lowered it. "I'm sorry. Is that what's wrong? Sebastian said you didn't want to marry him. But if—"

"It isn't Lord Sebastian." She found the handkerchief in her pocket and dabbed her eyes.

"Then who has made you cry."

"My father."

"Oh. Well, there isn't much I can do about that."

"He's angry. I...I'm in love with a man who will never have Father's approval."

Amanda's eyes grew wide. "You're in love? Eliza Southwick, I had no idea."

Legs weak, Eliza went to a chair and sat. "Neither did I. Not for certain until...until today."

"Who is he?" Amanda sat in a matching chair.

Tears welled in Eliza's eyes again. The room went silent for a long while. And then Amanda released a soft gasp. Eliza looked up.

"Adam?"

Eliza meant to shake her head, to lie, but she couldn't.

"You're in love with Adam."

Finally, she nodded.

"But that's wonderful."

"Wonderful?"

"Of course. Because I'm rather sure he feels very much the same about you."

"I don't think so." Eliza wiped her eyes again. "Not now. I...I hurt him. I said something I shouldn't have said."

Amanda smiled gently. "You couldn't hurt him if he didn't care. And the Adam I know is a very forgiving person."

The words brought a flicker of hope. Could that be true? She'd hurt him. At the very least, she'd wounded his pride. Would he still care for her after that? Would he forgive her?

"Eliza, I have never been in love, and no man has ever declared his love for me. At least not seriously. So I cannot claim to be an expert on matters of the heart. But I know Adam Faulkner. He is not a man to be easily dissuaded. If you have won his affections, then you will keep them, no matter what."

ADAM SAT ON A LARGE STONE, part of the crumbled remains of an ancient tower. Time had covered everything with vines and moss. The surrounding woods on this northern side of the Whitcombe estate were silent as they pressed in upon the site. In a couple of months, spring would awaken the trees. Birds and forest creatures would return to their branches. But for now, Adam and his horse were alone in nature's sanctuary. He'd discovered this place as a young boy and had continued to come here through the years whenever he needed solitude. It was a good place to think and to pray.

And he needed to do both.

It didn't surprise him that Eliza had questioned his motives. After all, it was no secret that the earl's interest in a match between Sebastian and Eliza had been more about her stallion than Eliza herself or even her dowry. Given his position as manager of the Whitcombe stables, the attention he'd paid to Eliza could be suspect. Another man might have had less than noble intentions.

"I've never told her I love her."

Only two days ago, he hadn't been willing to admit his feelings to himself. He hadn't understood how deep they went, so no wonder he hadn't been able to admit the depth to someone else. He also hadn't spoken with Eliza about his place in the Whitcombe family. Yes, she'd known from the start that he wasn't a legitimate son. But if he meant to ask her to leave the world of proper society to be with him, live on the edges that were allowed to him, shouldn't he explain it all? Didn't he need to discuss it openly and honestly with her?

"I shouldn't have left her in the chapel. We should have talked about it then and there."

The gray gelding lifted his head.

"I've made a mess of it."

The horse huffed, then returned to grazing.

"I do love her. I started to love her the night we met at Briar Park, and I will love her more the longer I know her." He drew in a long breath and released it. "But I want what is best for her, even above my own desires."

Elbows on his thighs, he hid his face in his hands and prayed for the strength and knowledge to do God's will.

Eliza pressed her face against Miss Dorset's neck, breathing in the horsey scent of the bay. "Where is he?" she whispered.

Adam hadn't joined his family and their guests for the midday meal nor had he made an appearance when some of the men decided to go shooting. Tired of waiting, she'd slipped away from her father's watchful eye and come to the stables, hoping to find Adam there, but the barn was empty except for horses. She supposed the stablehands were taking their well-earned sabbath rest, short though it might be. Horses had to be fed and watered, no matter the day of the week.

She drew back and stared into the mare's dark brown eyes. "You understand, don't you?"

The horse huffed, as if in response.

A few moments later, she heard the muffled sound of

hooves entering the stables. Her pulse quickened, but she couldn't seem to turn away from Miss Dorset and her understanding gaze.

"Eliza." Adam's soft voice coiled around her heart. "Miss Southwick."

At last she faced him. "Mr. Faulkner." She drew a breath. "Adam."

His tender gaze caressed her face as he stepped into the mare's stall.

"I owe you an apology," she said.

"No, you don't."

"Yes, I do. I know better than to believe you would…that you would try to court me in order to bring Glenhaven to your stables. You aren't that kind of man."

"They aren't my stables. But you're right. I wouldn't court you for that reason."

Her pulse fluttered, and she lowered her gaze to the floor. "Is there a reason you would court me?" She spoke the question so softly she didn't expect him to hear. Wasn't sure she wanted him to hear.

He heard. "Several reasons, Miss Southwick."

His reply drew her eyes to him once again.

"But before I tell you what they are, you should be aware of the reasons you *shouldn't* want me to court you." He took a step closer. "You know my…family history."

"Yes."

"Lord Whitcombe has always been kind to me. Fatherly to a degree, although not the same as with his lawful children. His wife, the late Lady Whitcombe, made the manor feel like home. In truth, Sebastian and Amanda think of me as their brother."

As they should since you are.

"But not everyone in society is as accepting as the Whitcombes. Because of their support, I have been allowed some privileges that most baseborn sons would not experience."

She wanted to object to his use of the term but pressed her lips together to keep from it.

"If I were to marry, my wife would never have the same admittance into society that Lady Amanda has. If I were to marry a woman of quality—" he took another step toward her "—she would have a very different life from the one she'd known before."

"What if she didn't like the life she'd known before?"

"Perhaps thinking about what she would have to give up would allow her to appreciate it more."

It was Eliza's turn to take a step forward. "Perhaps she is a thinking kind of woman. Perhaps she's had a number of years to think about it already and knows what matters to her."

"Eliza," he whispered, reaching out to brush her cheek with his fingers.

"Would now be the time for you to tell me the several reasons you have to court me?"

"Because I saw the look on your face when that foal was born in the Briar Park stables."

"Hmm."

One more step brought him close enough to take her in his arms. He didn't embrace her. Instead, he leaned forward, his forehead pressing against hers.

"Because," he continued, "I have witnessed your kindness to others."

She closed her eyes. "Mmm."

"Because I cherish the sound of your laughter and discovered that what amuses me also amuses you."

"Yes."

"Because when I think of spending the rest of my life with someone, the only someone I can picture is you."

Her breath caught. "Is that true?"

He drew his head back, and she opened her eyes.

He smiled. "That's true."

She released the air in her lungs and smiled back at him. "It's true for me as well."

His expression sobered as he leaned close once again. But it wasn't their foreheads that met. It was their mouths, his lips upon hers, warm and powerful and gentle and demanding, all at the same time. Her knees grew weak, and she was grateful for his arm that reached around and drew her closer still.

Chapter Twelve

Lord George's appearance in the stables early Monday morning didn't surprise Adam. He'd known it would happen eventually. He just hadn't thought it would be this soon. What had Eliza said to her father last night? Had she told him what happened in the barn?

"Faulkner."

"Lord George."

The man tugged at the collar of his great coat. "My daughter and I will be leaving this morning. Have my carriage ready by ten."

That wasn't what Adam had expected to hear. Not now. Not yet. "My lord." He cleared his throat. "I understood Lord Whitcombe expected all of his guests to remain for this evening's festivities."

"A waste of time to stay," Southwick muttered. "She'll do nothing but stand against the wall to watch others. That's all she ever does at balls and gatherings of all kinds."

Adam's gut clenched, and although it was tempting to say something in Eliza's defense, he managed to remain silent.

Southwick glared at him. "Is it true that more guests are expected?"

"Yes, my lord. Lady Amanda told me a party of twenty are coming for the dancing. Carriages will be sent to the train station to collect them later this morning."

"Waste of time," Eliza's father repeated.

Did the man think no one would be interested in his daughter? Did he not understand how desirable she was, how unique she was?

"Were you told who will be among the new arrivals?"

Adam supposed Southwick wanted to know if any dukes, marquises, or earls would be in the mix. Or at least more men who would eventually inherit one of those titles.

"Speak up, man," Southwick snapped.

"Sorry, my lord. Lady Amanda didn't say."

"Of course she didn't. Why would she tell you?"

And there, very clearly, was one of the reasons Eliza shouldn't accept his courtship.

"Very well." Eliza's father turned. "We won't leave until tomorrow. I suppose a miracle could happen tonight. Miserable day to travel anyway." He strode away without a backward glance.

Adam moved to a wood bench placed between two stall doors. Had he done the right thing yesterday, letting Eliza know how much he cared for her? Was he being fair to her? Given time, would she find someone else who could make her happy, a man who needn't apologize for his birth?

He shook his head. He didn't feel the need to apologize for his birth, although men like Southwick wanted him to. Instead he remembered the wisdom of Lady Whitcombe.

"God formed you, Adam," she had often told him when he was a boy. "You may have surprised Lord Whitcombe. You may have surprised your mother. But you weren't a surprise to God. You are special in His sight. Remember that when others are unkind and blame you for the circumstances of your birth. God the Father loves you. And so do I."

Silently, he thanked God once more for Lady Whitcombe. She had been a mother to him, the only mother he remembered. She could have resented him, hated him, sent him away, but she hadn't.

And now there was another woman who loved him. What was the best way for him to return that love?

———

Eliza awakened to daylight slipping past the heavy curtains of the bedchamber. It took only a moment to realize she was smiling. She'd probably smiled all night in her sleep.

Adam Faulkner loved her. While he hadn't said those exact words, she knew that's what he'd meant before he kissed her. He'd warned her why she shouldn't want him as a husband. He'd given her time to consider all of the ramifications of making such a choice. She'd told him none of those consequences would matter to her, but still he'd given her time to consider.

"However, they will matter to Father," she whispered.

The words caused her smile to deflate.

She didn't have to wonder what her father would do when she told him of her feelings for Adam. He'd already told her. He would disown her if she didn't marry a man of his choosing. Eliza's role in life was to marry well. Since Lord George, the third son of the Marquis of Heathborough, hadn't inherited a title of his own, it was important to him that Eliza marry into one. It would never occur to him that she didn't care about such things. Even if she told him plainly, he wouldn't believe it. A title mattered to him, ergo it must matter to her.

With a sigh, she tossed aside the blankets on the bed and slipped into her dressing gown. She considered ringing for a pot of hot chocolate but sounds from the antechamber stopped her. What on earth was Mary doing so early in the day? She crossed to the door and opened it.

"Mary, what on earth?"

Her maid looked up from the trunk she was wrestling with, startled. "I'm sorry, Miss Eliza. Did I wake you?"

"No. But what are you doing?"

"Packing, miss. Lord George says we are to leave this morning. We're going back to Briar Park."

"But we aren't supposed to leave for two more days.

There's to be a dance tonight. More guests are expected. Lady Amanda told us last night at supper."

Mary gave her an apologetic look. "His lordship sent word early this morning to say we are leaving."

Cold shivered through Eliza. Cold that had nothing to do with the temperature of the bedchamber. Had Father guessed who at Hooke Manor had drawn her interest? Had he seen her returning from the stables yesterday, cheeks flushed and joy exploding in her heart?

"Stop packing, Mary. I am not leaving today."

"But Miss Eliza, his lordship said——"

"I'm not leaving and neither are you. Not yet."

A rap came at the hall door, and Mary went to answer it. When she returned, she wore a puzzled expression. "How did you know, miss?"

Eliza shook her head, not understanding the question.

"The footman brought a message from your father. He said we will not leave today after all."

Eliza frowned. Why had her father changed his mind? That was unlike him. He was a man of singular focus, and when he'd decided on a course of action, that was that.

She returned to the bedchamber where she pushed aside the draperies, letting in anemic morning light. A curtain of fog wove through trees and bushes and obscured the expansive grounds. Perhaps the weather was the reason for her father changing his departure plans. Fog and cold would make for a miserable journey home.

"Will you go down for breakfast or take it here, Miss Eliza?"

"I'll go down." She turned from the window.

"Would you like the blue and white gown or the burgundy?"

She didn't really care what she wore, but she knew her maid needed her to choose something. "The burgundy, I think."

"That's my favorite, miss. It brings out the color in your cheeks."

Affection for the servant warmed Eliza, and that, in turn, brought renewed hope for the day that lay ahead.

She'd fallen in love with Adam Faulkner because he saw her. He didn't see a dowry. He didn't see a fine horse to add to his—or the earl's—stables. He saw *her*. And in turn, she saw him. Others might think him of ignoble birth, but she saw the man he was. A man of honor. A man who cared for others. A man who was tender and giving. When she imagined a future with him, it was a future with meaning and purpose.

She stopped still as a memory came to her. The night of the Blakeslee Ball when she'd asked God to send the right man into her life. *Please send me someone to love*, she'd prayed. Even then, she'd remembered her first encounter with Adam, although she hadn't known he would be the answer to her prayer.

Now she knew.

Chapter Thirteen

"Father, I need to speak with you."

Eliza entered the library, glad she'd found her father alone. No doubt he had come here to escape the noisy conversations in other rooms. After the arrival of two dozen more guests, it wasn't easy to find a quiet place, not even in a house as large as Hooke Manor.

"And I need to speak to you." Her father rose from the chair.

"Please allow me to go first."

He scowled his displeasure.

"Lady Amanda has invited me to extend my visit until the London Season begins, and I would like to stay."

"For what purpose?"

"Does there have to be a purpose?" She closed her eyes, knowing she'd asked the question to give herself more time to find the right words. Looking at him again, she said, "I would like to stay. I would like to spend more time with...with my friend."

He cocked an eyebrow. "Friend. Since when is Lady Amanda your friend? She was little more than an acquaintance before our arrival. Besides, you don't need a friend. You need a husband. If Lord Sebastian was inclined to change his mind about you, maybe there would be value in a longer stay. But as it is—"

"Father, I *am* going to stay."

His face reddened, and his cheeks puffed out.

"Please understand. There…there is a good reason for me to remain here."

"Balderdash!"

Eliza drew herself up and leveled her shoulders. It was time to speak plainly. It was time to tell him *why* Amanda Whitcombe had extended her invitation. She'd done it for Eliza and Adam. She was helping them have more time together. "Father, I—"

The library door burst open, accompanied by unrestrained laughter. Two women stumbled into the room, giggling, followed by three gentlemen. They drew up short when they saw Eliza and her father.

"Pardon us," one of the men said before they left the library in a more decorous manner.

The door had barely clicked closed behind the intruders when her father said, "I'll hear no more of this. We will both depart on the morrow. Be assured of that. And if you have any sense, girl, you will make the most of your evening of dancing." Then he strode from the room.

Eliza moved to the nearest chair and sank onto it. "That didn't go as planned."

As silence enveloped her, a shadow of doubt crossed her mind. What if she chose to stay with Adam, but he discovered he didn't really want to be with her, that his attraction had only been a passing fancy? What would become of her then?

As happened every now and then, she thought of the woman who had served as nanny to Eliza and her brother. A kindly woman with gray hair poking from beneath a white cap, the front of her black dress covered by a crisp, white apron, Nanny had left the Southwick employ once William went away to school. But Eliza still recalled the lessons the woman had taught them. This time, she remembered the story of the Israelites crossing the Jordan.

"The waters didn't part until they stepped into the water. That takes faith, Miss Eliza. Living takes faith."

As if in answer to the memory, sunlight spilled through the library window, puddling on the floor at her feet. The fog had lifted and the day was suddenly bright.

"I'll have faith." She stood. "I'll step into the water, believing it will part."

———

THE SUN WAS ALREADY low in the west as Adam mounted his horse and cantered in the direction of Hooke Manor. He would be lucky to arrive before the dancing started.

Of course, when he'd made the appointment with the stable manager at Thornton House, Adam hadn't planned to participate in any of the Whitcombe festivities during their house party. But last night, Sebastian had sought him out, insisting that Adam join them this evening. It would have been easier to refuse. Few of those present would want him there. But he found himself unable to decline the invitation. He wanted to be with Eliza tonight, to dance with her, to let anyone with eyes—including her father—see that he was claiming her for his own.

Throughout this day—from the moment Southwick had come to the stables to conducting his business at Thornton House to the present moment as twilight fell over the countryside—Eliza had been in Adam's thoughts. He remembered the sweet kisses they'd shared in the barn. He remembered the way her long, dark eyelashes looked against her smooth skin when she closed her eyes. He remembered the delicate scent of her cologne.

He didn't want to admit—not even to himself—how much it would hurt if she changed her mind, if she decided being with him wouldn't be worth the losses she would suffer. But there was no going back now. He'd given her this day to test her heart. Tonight he would seek her answer.

He pressed his heels against the gelding's sides, urging more speed.

Destiny awaited him in the grand salon of Hooke Manor.

WEARING a beaded satin evening gown in her favorite shade of red, Eliza stood near a window. Close enough to feel the cool night air upon the exposed skin of her back and arms. The grand salon and drawing room had been cleared of most of the furniture, providing plenty of space for the dancers as they swept around the floor and from room to room, utilizing connecting doorways at both ends of the two rooms. The trio of musicians—with their cello, violin, and viola—had been stationed on the first landing of the staircase, overlooking the grand salon.

As the lively two-step ended, Sebastian walked toward Eliza. He smiled as he came to a halt. "Miss Southwick, may I have the pleasure of the next dance?"

Her heart squeezed in her chest. What she really wanted was to slip away to a private room to cry. Adam hadn't come. And her heart ached for him. She fought back the tears of disappointment and forced her own smile. "I would like that very much, Lord Sebastian."

She glanced away from him and discovered her father watching from the opposite side of the room. Earlier when she'd seen him, his brow had been furrowed in a scowl, but now he looked more surprised than anything else.

The musicians began to play again, a Viennese waltz this time.

Sebastian bowed before reaching for her hand.

"Would I be allowed to cut in before you even begin?" Adam stepped close, looking from her to his half-brother.

Eliza's pulse leapt and her throat went dry. He was here. He'd come.

Sebastian took a step back. "Of course." He grinned.

"Miss Southwick, shall we dance?"

She nodded, unable to speak. This was the moment. She didn't need to look at her father again to know. This was her Jordan River moment.

I'm stepping in, Lord.

Adam reached out with his left hand and took hold of her right. Despite both of them wearing gloves, she felt his warmth, like a hot stone beneath the blankets. A moment later, his right hand touched the small of her back. With an expertise she hadn't expected, he drew her into the midst of dancers.

"I'm sorry I was late," he said. "I was away from the estate for most of the day."

She barely heard him above the pounding of her heart.

"Your father is watching us."

"I know."

"So are others."

"I don't care."

"Sebastian and Amanda are pleased. I believe we may consider them our champions."

The words made her want to laugh. Perhaps anything he said would make her want to laugh at this point. She was giddy with happiness.

"I spoke to Lord Whitcombe before joining the festivities."

Her step faltered, but Adam's hand on her waist steadied her.

"He seems to think, if I were to marry, that a better position for me would be as estate manager. An estate manager who is still very involved with the Whitcombe stables. More responsibility, of course, and an increase in wages."

"If I were to marry..." It was hard to make sense of anything he'd said after those few words. "Adam, what are you saying?"

He danced her into a corner and stopped. His smile faded. His eyes grew serious. "I am saying—and saying it poorly, I fear—that I love you, Eliza Southwick. I'm saying that I don't want to live a moment without you. I'm asking you to be my wife. I'm asking you to come make your home at Hooke Manor in a cottage with me."

Just as soberly, she said, "My father will disown me. I will come without a dowry and without any hope of an inheritance."

"I don't want or need either of those things. All I need is you. I think I knew that the first night we met in the Briar Park stables."

"I think my heart knew it that night, too. It took a little longer for my mind to know it was real. Yes, I will marry you. I love you. Adam Faulkner, you are the answer to my prayers."

His eyes sparkled. Was it amusement or simply the reflection of lights in the room? "I've never been the answer to anyone's prayers before. It's rather nice."

"Mr. Faulkner—" her joy was difficult to contain,

though she did her best to look stern "—don't let it go to your head."

He laughed loudly, drawing gazes from around the room. Ignoring the onlookers, he took hold of her right hand once again and swirled her back onto the floor.

Eliza's heart sang, knowing they would dance through life together, forever as close as they were now.

Epilogue

Faulkner Cottage, Hooke Manor Estate
Spring 1895

Eliza removed her apron, then used her hands to tidy her hair before leaving the cottage. The afternoon was sunny, and she needed nothing more than a light shawl about her shoulders to keep warm on the walk to the stables.

She paused halfway to her destination and turned her face toward the sky, happiness fluttering in her chest. Sometimes she wanted to pinch herself to see if her life was real or if she were dreaming.

Not that everything over the last couple of months had been easy. As promised, her father had disowned her, turning her out. She'd taken her clothes, the jewelry that had been her mother's, her maid—now employed in the manor house—and Glenhaven, and she'd walked away from the place that had been her home her entire life. She'd left behind family and friends, knowing she would never see most of them again.

On the other hand, she'd been warmly welcomed into the Whitcombe family. Even the earl made her feel at home. And, of course, there was Adam. His love made up for anything she'd left behind.

Eliza and Adam had married in the Hooke Manor chapel on the first day of April. The affair had been small and intimate, just as Eliza preferred, and the days and weeks that followed had brought more happiness than she'd known since her mother died.

"Thank You," she whispered before resuming her walk to the stables.

Inside the barn, she found her husband, along with his half-siblings and Roger Bernhardt, all of them observing Miss Dorset as the mare was walked by a groom around the arena.

"She's with foal," Adam said. "I'd wager money on it."

"Too soon to be sure," Sebastian countered. "But you always did have a nose for such things."

Eliza stepped to Adam's side. "He may have a nose about horses, but he is useless when it comes to keeping track of time." She slipped an arm through his. "Aren't you hungry? Your midday meal has grown cold waiting for you."

"Sorry. I didn't notice the time. But don't pretend you aren't as excited as I am about the possibility of a Glenhaven foal out of Miss Dorset."

"I'm not pretending any such thing. I simply think you should eat when the food is ready." She kissed

Adam on the cheek. "Or is it my lack of cooking skills that keeps you away from the table?"

"Never," he said in a low voice, the kind that made her toes curl.

"Gracious." Amanda laughed softly. "You two make me a little envious of your domestic bliss."

Sebastian elbowed his sister. "Want me to find you a husband?"

"Never."

"Never?"

"I'll do what Eliza did," Amanda answered with a bright smile. "I'll choose my own husband when the time comes. No one—including you or Father—will do the choosing for me."

"We don't always get to choose what we want," Sebastian said, his voice serious, "or when we want it or even who we want."

Amanda touched her brother's forearm. "You're worried about the promise you made Father."

Eliza looked between the siblings. "What promise?"

Amanda answered, "He promised, if Father allowed us to spend a year in America, that he will find a woman to marry within another year after our return to England."

"Do you have someone in mind?" Adam asked.

Sebastian frowned. "No."

Adam leaned close to Eliza's ear. "Between the two of us, we can think of someone for him."

She laughed as she stepped back and tugged on Adam's hand. "Come with me. We can consider all the possibilities while we eat."

Adam shrugged as he sent a helpless look in Sebastian and Amanda's direction, making Eliza laugh. Then he accompanied her out into the bright light of day.

"You know," he said when they were halfway to the cottage, "a perfect woman isn't all that easy to find."

"She doesn't have to be perfect, Adam." Eliza stopped walking and turned into his waiting embrace. "She only has to be perfect for Sebastian."

"The way you are for me," he said softly. "And I am for you."

"Mmm." It was the only reply she managed as his lips claimed hers in a kiss that made Eliza forget everything except the man who held her close.

Perfect, indeed.

***

The British Are Coming to America. Keep reading to learn more.

THE BRITISH ARE COMING series begins with *To Enchant a Lady's Heart,* a novella set in Victorian England, where readers meet Adam Faulkner, the illegitimate son of the Earl of Hooke, and the gentlewoman he loves.

It continues with three novels set in America in the mid-1890s featuring Sebastian Whitcombe, heir to the Earl of Hooke; his younger sister, Lady Amanda Whitcombe; and his tradesman friend, Roger Bernhardt. They have come to the American West —Sebastian for a last adventure before taking himself a wife, Amanda to experience some of the thrills she witnessed as a child in London at Buffalo Bill's Wild West show, and Roger to paint the beauty of Yellowstone before taking over the family business in London. Adventure and romance abound!

TURN THE PAGE FOR A PEEK
AT SEBASTIAN'S STORY
COMING IN FALL 2023

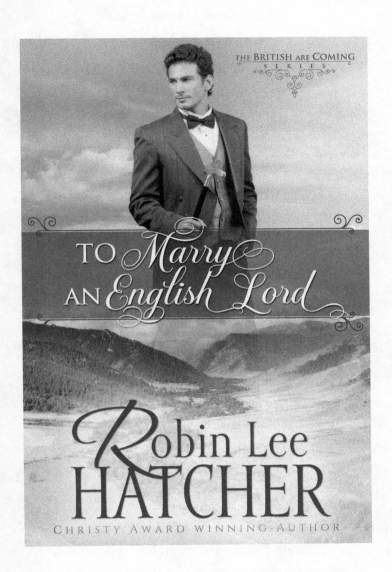

THE BRITISH ARE COMING
SERIES

TO Marry AN English Lord

Robin Lee HATCHER

CHRISTY AWARD WINNING AUTHOR

TO MARRY AN ENGLISH LORD
The British Are Coming, Book 2
by
Robin Lee Hatcher

PROLOGUE

New York City
April 1895

"Miss Overstreet, is something wrong?"

Jocelyn looked from the telegram in her hand to her assistant who stood in the doorway of her office. "Yes, Mr. Danvers." She removed her reading spectacles. "My brother has been seriously injured. Mrs. Adler didn't say what happened, just that I am needed. Please make arrangements for me to leave on the train tomorrow."

"Pocatello?" Paul Danvers watched her expectantly, pencil and paper in hand.

"Yes. And hire me a coach from there to the ranch."

With a nod, Paul left, pulling the door closed behind him.

Jocelyn sighed as she rose from her desk and went to the windows overlooking the Hudson River. When she was a little girl, she'd loved to accompany her father, Alexander Overstreet, to this office. She'd listened and observed and absorbed as he read reports and made decisions and shouted at employees. Everything about this place had seemed exciting to her.

Of course, her brother William—or Billy as she still called him—had been destined to take over the reins when their father passed on. Only William hadn't wanted anything to do with Overstreet Shipping. By his early twenties, he'd had his fill of New York and London and sailing in between those two cities. His heart had been set on the Idaho cattle ranch, their mother's inheritance. And so, out of desperation, their father had left the running of Overstreet Shipping to Jocelyn.

In the eight years since their father's passing, she'd learned both to love and despise the business that occupied so much of her life. Perhaps a few weeks spent on the family ranch would bring her some perspective.

CHAPTER ONE

Eden's Gate Ranch, Idaho
May 1895

Sebastian Whitcombe, Viscount Willowthorpe, reined in the gelding at the top of the rise and waited for the coach to catch up to him.

Before the vehicle stopped, his sister's head poked out the open window. "What is it? More buffalo?"

"No, Amanda. We are almost to our destination. There it is." He pointed. "Our home for the coming year. Eden's Gate Ranch."

The coach door opened, and Roger Bernhardt, Sebastian's close friend, stepped to the ground. Then he turned and helped Amanda do the same. On the opposite side of a deep, verdant valley sat a stone house. It was large by most standards, though not when compared to Hooke Manor, seat of the earls of Hooke for more than three centuries.

"Breathtaking," Roger said.

Sebastian grinned. If Roger had his way, he would pull out canvas and paints and get to work capturing the spectacular mountain peaks that rose behind the ranch house.

"Do you suppose we could enjoy the view later?" Amanda asked, a touch of petulance in her voice. "I'm famished, and it's been a long day already."

"I'm hungry myself," Sebastian replied. "Let's hope the cook is ready for us. I did hire a man to go ahead of us to alert William of our arrival, but I wasn't sure how long the journey would take."

Roger turned in a slow circle, taking in the view from all directions. "How long has it been since you've seen this chap?"

"William? About seven or eight years, I think. Whenever he was last in England. He was supposed to take over his family's shipping business from his father. But when the time came, he turned his back on it and moved to this cattle ranch. Never looked back. Lucky fellow, getting to make his own choice."

"Is he the reason you were so set on this trip?"

Sebastian smiled. "Maybe. When we were at school together, he had a way of describing this ranch, this whole country, that made me eager to see it for myself. I'd say he delivered on his promises."

Roger made a sound of agreement before helping Amanda into the coach, and the small party rode on at a brisk pace.

Sebastian had known before leaving England that America was a large country, but he hadn't been prepared for the sheer vastness of it. Or for the ever-changing beauty. Like this valley in the shadow of the rugged Rocky Mountains. The next year would be amazing. He had no doubt about it.

And then—he frowned as he remembered what would follow his year in America—he would return to England, marry a girl who met with his father's approval, and do his duty to provide an heir. As the earl liked to remind him, Sebastian wasn't getting any younger. At thirty-two, it was time for him to settle down and learn to run Hooke Manor and the other estates belonging to the Whitcombe family.

"I won't live forever," his father liked to say.

Maybe not forever, but judging by Edward Whitcombe's robust health, for a good many more years to come.

Half an hour later, the Whitcombe party arrived at their destination. The exterior of the large ranch house was made of fieldstone of gray, white, and gold. L-shaped, it had three stories and an abundance of windows. They would hardly be roughing it for the coming year.

Sebastian dismounted and looped the reins around a post. He was about to turn to the coach when the front door opened and a portly woman in a black dress stepped onto the veranda, frowning, as if their arrival displeased her.

"Good day, madam," he said. "I am Sebastian Whitcombe. I believe you are expecting us."

"Indeed, Mr. Whitcombe. I am Mrs. Adler. The housekeeper."

Sebastian glanced at the land that was dotted with brown cattle. "Is Mr. Overstreet around?"

"Yes, sir. But he's not able to come to see you. I'm afraid there's been an accident."

"An accident?" His gaze shot back to the woman. "Is it serious?"

"Serious enough." She drew herself up, her look disapproving. "And because of you lot, he's staying in the guesthouse."

Sebastian wasn't used to a servant speaking to him in such a manner. How was he supposed to respond to her?

"Is something wrong?" Amanda asked softly from behind him.

He turned to his sister and Roger. "It would seem so. William's had some sort of accident."

"Come with me." Mrs. Adler's words were more command than invitation. "Might as well get you settled."

———

Six years had passed since Jocelyn's last visit to Eden's Gate. The demands of Overstreet Shipping always seemed greater than her desire to return to Idaho or to spend time with her brother, despite how much she loved him.

But now, looking out of the coach window at the terrain—pale green grasses waving in a breeze, the Teton Range to the east resplendent in its rocky majesty—she wondered how she'd let so much time go by. She loved this country. She loved the ranch. She loved riding horses and herding cattle. She loved sitting by the fire and telling stories. She loved the changing seasons, seasons that were distinct, seasons that could be harsh even while beautiful.

Leaning back against the seat, Jocelyn closed her eyes and sent up a quick prayer for William. She didn't know how serious his injuries were, but they must be grave. Otherwise, Mrs. Adler wouldn't have sent for her.

But what awaited her at Eden's Gate? Were his

injuries permanent? Would he walk again or see again or speak again? Her heart stuttered. Had he died before she could reach the ranch? Had she come too late?

The coach slowed as it began a slow descent. She opened her eyes, but she already knew what she would see. She had lived most of her life in the East. She knew the streets of Manhattan and the docks along the Hudson as well as she knew her own name. But her heart came alive in this Idaho valley, and she found herself hoping that William would need her to stay a long while.

Jocelyn leaned forward on the seat, as if it would hurry the horses pulling the coach to her destination. And when they did arrive, she didn't wait for the driver to get down from his perch and open the door for her. She opened it herself—even as the coach rocked back and forth—and jumped to the ground.

Lifting the skirt of her travel dress, she ran to the front door of the stone house. Opening it, she called, "William! Mrs. Adler!"

Receiving no reply, she hurried toward the stairs. As she rounded a corner, she ran into a man's broad chest.

"By heaven!" He caught her by the shoulders, steadying her.

He was a tall man, a stranger to her, and by his dress she knew he wasn't one of her brother's cowboys.

"May I be of some assistance?" he asked.

Tilting her head up to meet his gaze, she took a step back. Out of his reach. "Who are you?" she demanded. "What are you doing in this house?"

"I am Sebastian Whitcombe. I live here for the time

being." He cocked an imperious brow. "And who, might I ask, are you?"

Jocelyn took another step back. She was about to answer when she heard a familiar voice speak her name. She turned to face the Eden's Gate housekeeper. "Mrs. Adler." Relief rushed through her. "I came as soon as I received the telegram." She cast a glance over her shoulder at the stranger, then returned her eyes to the older woman. "Where is Billy?"

"He's in the guesthouse, Miss Joss. He'll be glad to see you."

The guesthouse? Why was her brother in the guest-house? What was wrong with his room? Was he conta-gious? And who was this man who claimed to live in this house? *Her* house.

To Marry an English Lord
Fall 2023

https://robinleehatcher.com

Subscribe to the Robin's Notes newsletter to stay informed about new and upcoming releases and sales on her other books.

About the Author

Robin Lee Hatcher is the best-selling author of over 85 books. Her well-drawn characters and heartwarming stories of faith, courage, and love have earned her both critical acclaim and the devotion of readers. Her numerous awards include the Christy Award for Excellence in Christian Fiction, the RITA® Award for Best Inspirational Romance, Romantic Times Career Achievement Awards for Americana Romance and for Inspirational Fiction, the Carol Award, the 2011 Idahope Writer of the Year, and Lifetime Achievement Awards from both Romance Writers of America® (2001) and American Christian Fiction Writers (2014). *Catching Katie* was named one of the Best Books of 2004 by the Library Journal.

When not writing, Robin enjoys being with her family, spending time in the beautiful Idaho outdoors, Bible art journaling, reading books that make her cry, watching romantic movies, knitting, and decorative planning. A mother and grandmother, Robin makes her home on the outskirts of Boise, sharing it with a demanding Papillon dog and a persnickety tuxedo cat.

Learn more about Robin and her books by visiting her website at robinleehatcher.com

You can also find out more by joining her on Facebook, Twitter, or Instagram.

Acknowledgments

The idea for The British Are Coming series first came to me in 2009. The books were supposed to have a couple of different homes over the years, but life happened and the stories stayed in my idea file. Then came January of 2022, when I was wondering what I wanted to write after I finished *All She Ever Dreamed*. I knew the instant I looked in my idea file that the time had come for these stories to be born.

First, I have to thank Tamera Alexander for the great brainstorming we did together in 2009/2010. It remains distinct in my mind, and your enthusiasm for these stories has stayed with me as well.

Many, many thanks to my literary agent. Natasha, we had 33 amazing years together. I am so grateful for your expertise and your encouragement through all of the ups and downs of publishing. But I am even more thankful for our friendship.

As always, I can't imagine doing life without my wonderful sisters in Christ who meet every summer in beautiful Coeur d'Alene. You have prayed me through so much, my friends. May God repay you a hundred-fold for your faithfulness.

And finally, thanks to my wonderful family. I love each and every one of you. The more the merrier!

Also by
Robin Lee Hatcher

Stand Alone Titles

Like the Wind

I'll Be Seeing You

Words Matter

Make You Feel My Love

An Idaho Christmas

Here in Hart's Crossing

The Victory Club

Beyond the Shadows

Catching Katie

Whispers From Yesterday

The Shepherd's Voice

Ribbon of Years

Firstborn

The Forgiving Hour

Heart Rings

A Wish and a Prayer

When Love Blooms

A Carol for Christmas

Return to Me

Loving Libby

Wagered Heart

The Perfect Life

Speak to Me of Love

Trouble in Paradise

Another Chance to Love You

Bundle of Joy

The British Are Coming

To Enchant a Lady's Heart

Boulder Creek Romance

Even Forever

All She Ever Dreamed

The Coming to America Series

Dear Lady

Patterns of Love

In His Arms

Promised to Me

Where the Heart Lives Series

Belonging

Betrayal

Beloved

Books set in Kings Meadow

A Promise Kept

Love Without End

Whenever You Come Around

I Hope You Dance

Keeper of the Stars

Books set in Thunder Creek

You'll Think of Me

You're Gonna Love Me

The Sisters of Bethlehem Springs Series

A Vote of Confidence

Fit to Be Tied

A Matter of Character

Legacy of Faith series

Who I am With You

Cross My Heart

How Sweet It Is

For a full list of books, visit robinleehatcher.com